Thirst

A Novel of
Lost Innocence
And Redemption

H. W. Terrance

Published by YourBookTeam.com
First edition
Editors: Emily Sanfilippo, Sydney Scalia, Jordan Nicole, Jowanah
Majeed, Genevieve Cramer, Ilana Krebs, Ray Hazenstab, and
John Kiss.
For permissions requests, contact:
www.YourBookTeam.com

Note to the Reader

This novel contains themes and content that may be sensitive or upsetting to some readers. This includes the following:

Misogyny: Themes of misogyny appear and are critically analyzed within the narrative. These depictions are intended to emphasize trauma, and the results of such trauma. It is not intended to glorify the behavior, only to point out the character's struggle to evolve. This may be upsetting for some readers.

Sexually Explicit Content: Certain chapters of the book include sexually explicit content and reader discretion is advised.

Transgender Individuals: the story contains transgender individuals. While the author has attempted to address these topics with care and respect, there may be depictions and themes that some readers will find offensive or disturbing.

Readers are encouraged to consider their sensitivities to these subjects before proceeding. The author hopes to foster knowledge and dialogue about these behaviors, and appreciates your tolerance of these complicated subjects.

Author's Note

An alcoholic in his cups is an unlovely creature. Many of the descriptions of the behavior shared in this novel are difficult to relate to. The addict/alcoholic is a person driven by instincts, and very little morality. This is a disease of the mind as much as it is an allergy of the body. The mind is sick. Fixated with extreme self centeredness. Egocentric. The idea that this person is one among many, or part of the collective society, is void in their consciousness. They are driven by a thousand forms of fear: self-centered fear. They make their way through life grasping for more of what they think makes them happy, safe, or important with no regard for the effect it has on others. This is the heart-breaking reality of addiction. This lovable person becomes unlovable over time, when their true motives are exposed. Innocent people become victims of these unfeeling monsters. The only chance that the monsters can return to their rightful place amongst their family, friends and society, is through a complete psychological transformation. This book explores that journey.

"Every saint has a past, and every sinner has a future"

— *Oscar Wilde*

Prologue

Late November in the Great White North was cold enough to freeze the balls off a brass monkey. Just a regular night, but by the end of it, someone was getting locked up.

The Hound and his friends went to Quebec to see the Montreal Canadians hockey game at the Forum. No one was old enough to drive, so the boys took the bus.

At the back of the bus, they each had twelve stubbies of Labatt Blue, 12 ounces of beer in short, fat bottles. They drank them all on the trip. The Hound was young and cheap, and decided to keep his empties—after all, he could get 10 cents a bottle!

Off the bus they stumbled, the Hound carrying his Adidas bag full of empty beer bottles. They walked the block to the Forum to watch the game and drank draft beer from plastic cups all night, becoming even more drunk. When the game ended, the Hound didn't care who won. He was too drunk to even notice.

They walked the streets until it was time to catch the last bus home. The guys hurried to the bus station. They were rowdy, and the Hound's friend Smith—whose mom was French—started yelling french swear words at everyone. "*Tabarnak*, you French bastards!"

Nobody was impressed. Even the Hound warned him. "Shut up Smith, we're in Quebec! You're gonna get us in shit!"

As the lads approached the bus, the bus driver seemed to be waiting for them, and prevented them from getting on. "I'm sorry, boys," he said in a French-Canadian accent. "You cannot get on my bus. You are too drunk."

The Hound stepped forward, outraged by the irony. "What are you talking about? We took the bus because we knew we were going to get drunk! We have to get back to Toronto, and this is the last bus!"

"I'm sorry," said the bus driver. "You can get a hotel."

The Hound switched his tactic. "I promise," he charmed with a smile. "We'll be good. We just want to go to the back of the bus and go to sleep."

"I don't trust you boys," said the bus driver. "You'll make trouble on my bus. No, you cannot come."

The Hound switched his tactic again. "We're getting on the fucking bus and *you* can't stop us."

With this, the Hound felt a hand on his shoulder. He knew it wasn't his friends as they were in front of him. *It must be somebody else*, he thought—*somebody that was gonna get it.*

The Hound gripped his Adidas bag tight and spun around, smashing the man in the head with all the empty beer bottles in the bag.

The man flew backwards, landing on the floor. Just then the Hound noticed the uniform.

Damn.

A policeman.

He had knocked him out cold. Before the Hound could look for an escape, five more policemen were encircling him. The Hound put his hands up as they tackled him to the floor.

They handcuffed him and took him to the back of the bus station, into a private office. They didn't want any witnesses.

They started to beat the Hound with their clubs and fists, but not to the face—they didn't want any evidence. The Hound took the beating and smiled. "Is that all you got?"

They beat him some more.

They took him to jail. Booking him in at the sergeant's desk. The Hound said, "I'll take the penthouse, preferably with a view."

Still standing in front of the desk sergeant, another man in handcuffs came crashing through the front door. Six policemen were trying to control him. He was a monster, had to be six-five, 260 pounds, and he had a ski mask on. As the policemen wrestled him up to the sergeant's desk he stood next to the Hound. The Hound was dwarfed by this giant.

While the six cops held him in place they ripped his ski mask off, revealing a hideous crazed-eyed looking monster, who slowly turned his head towards the Hound.

Their eyes met, and the man smiled at the Hound like he was about to eat him.

The Hound looked at the sergeant and pleaded, "Please don't put me in his cell!"

Soon, he was in a cage with fifteen other men that all looked like murderers. There was nowhere to sit, only a hole in the center of the floor for a toilet. These animals pissed and shit into a hole, in front of everybody. *This was not a five-star accommodation.*

The Hound put his back against the corner and stayed awake. *He wasn't in Kansas anymore.* These men were dangerous. A few sat quietly with a thousand-yard stare, but it was the restless ones he worried about. Walking back and forth, agitated, looking for a fight. Many of them had tattoos of demons and such. He reassured himself that they couldn't be armed, but he knew he was smaller than most of them.

No one was coming to save him tonight.

Maybe his dad was right, the Hound thought. *Maybe he was destined to be a ditch digger.*

The Hound sat quietly in his corner, reflecting on how far he had fallen. He wasn't always this way. When he was young, there was so much promise. Here he was, fifteen, and way off track.

How the hell did he get here?

1

Born to Be Wild

He was a good boy. An innocent boy. He was seven years old, a boy full of life and wonder. Adventure was his daily reprieve. He played hockey and baseball, and loved to walk across the park, balancing on the top of the wooden fence.

He'd go down to the creek and catch tadpoles and baby frogs. He loved hamburgers, and his favorite pop was root beer. He liked chips and chocolate bars, but he didn't think much of vegetables.

He was a born salesman: he would talk all the other kids into playing road hockey. Somehow, he instinctively knew that people were followers. So he'd tell each boy that the other boys were *already* playing, even though nobody had committed yet. And by the time he'd finish calling them all, the game was on.

The boy had to carry his hockey nets, one on each shoulder, walking on his tippy-toes, as the nets were almost as tall as him. He hiked that mile or two up to the tennis court, where they played hockey on one side of the net, across two courts. The boy loved hockey, maybe because he was *the best*. He always scored goals. It might not amount to anything, but as long as he could score goals, he didn't really care.

His older brother, Daniel, was twelve. Daniel was much taller, and read books every day. He told the boy a lot of things that he had learned from those books. Some of the things the boy believed, and some he didn't. But when the boy needed to know something, he asked his brother. He trusted him. He knew that he was a good person—just different.

They played sockwars in the hallway. They'd pile pillows up at each end of the hallway to hide behind, and have all their socks folded into balls to throw at each other. Throwing sock bombs at each other down the hallway was the closest they would ever get.

His dad was a military man, and apparently, quite a sportsman. He loved to be the hero at the bar, with his friends and his beer. The boy rarely saw him at night.

The boy's mother was always home. She did her best to feed the boys and make sure they had clothes, but she never said she loved them. She didn't believe in the word *love*.

The boy loved his mother, even though she was the saddest person he had ever known.

2

The Long and Winding Road

Saturday mornings were his favorite. He didn't have to go to school, and nobody else was watching TV. He eagerly turned on the cartoons and could hear Bugs Bunny's iconic "What's up, Doc?" as the Looney Tunes hour began. Then, he would head out to the backyard, to play with his dinky cars in the sandpit. He imagined great successes in his life, with his dream car being a Mercedes.

He always saw the birds, the bees, and the butterflies. He loved all of God's creatures. He was a hard worker, and was even given a paper route at the age of seven. After all, he knew that no one was gonna buy him that Mercedes.

He woke up at the crack of dawn, mounted his one-speed bicycle, and pedaled down to the local convenience store, where he picked up his 27 papers. He envied the boys with apartment routes. His customers were scattered across the county. Yet off he rode, rain or shine, to deliver his papers before school started.

He never felt discontented. Instead, he considered himself fortunate to have a job, and to enjoy the solitude of nature among the trees and flowers as he rode the country roads.

He was always seen talking to himself, and singing out loud. One day his mother asked him: "Who are you speaking to?"

"God, of course," he answered.

Though his mother was an atheist, she thought this was cute. The boy's faith was his own. Nobody in his family shared it—but *he* knew God was there.

One evening, he would get evidence of this in the most extraordinary way for him. He attended a banquet where all the hockey teams gathered to receive their year-end trophies. He had to get a ride from the neighbors because his parents never went out of the house at night once they were home. In fact, they never went to anything of his: no games, no school functions. The boy never felt the lack, he was too busy chasing his dreams.

That night, the boy walked in front of the tables full of trophies, until he found the table that had his league and his age group. His eyes fell upon the smallest trophy, which read: *Playing Ability And Sportsmanship*. He felt confident that he scored the most goals that year, and only had a few penalties.

The boy prayed under his breath, "Please, God, can I just have this *little* trophy? I think I earned it."

The boy went back to his table and sat down to eat his

dinner. All the other kids were talking with their parents. So he just sat quietly and ate. Soon, the awards were to be given. And when the announcer got to his age group, he called out the winner of Sportsmanship and Playing Ability:.... Our boy.

The boy jumped up to get the small trophy, eagerly approaching the man to shake his hand and receive the award. But to his astonishment, the man handed him a *huge* trophy: standing at least three feet tall, in addition to the little one.

Two trophies! One to keep forever, and one to put in his bedroom for the year, to show everyone this giant accomplishment.

After the banquet, he caught a ride home with their neighbor, Mrs. Stevens. "My, your parents are sure gonna be proud of you!" She remarked.

The boy wasn't convinced.

He burst through the back door yelling to his parents, "Look what I won, look what I won!"

His father was sitting in his chair, watching television. He gulped down his beer as he glanced over, unimpressed. "I've won lots of trophies," he said.

The boy's need for his father's approval would not be quenched tonight.

His mother tried to temper it: "Good job, son."

That was enough for the boy. He was not used to receiving much praise anyways. He took his trophies back to his room to bask in the glory of his victory. Reflecting on the generosity of God, who had let him win not only the small trophy, but also a giant one, four-times bigger than the one he had asked for!

The boy learned that day that if he worked hard for something, and became excellent at it, God would reward him far greater than he ever expected. That night, he believed in God more than ever.

3

You've Lost That Lovin' Feelin'

When Monday morning arrived and he returned to school, our boy beamed with confidence. He decided it was time he had a woman - after all, he was in grade five!

There could only be one girl for him: Trish. She was the cutest girl in class. *All the boys liked her.*

With his newfound confidence, he strutted over and invited her on a date.

To his surprise, she said "Yes!"

"Great," he said, "let's meet after school and you can come watch me play hockey."

The end of the school day came, and they held hands and headed to the rec center, where the floor hockey game took place every afternoon.

Our boy was so proud of having a girlfriend. He walked

into the gym, showing her off to all the other boys. He gestured to her, "You go wait over there and watch me play hockey. I'm pretty good, you know!"

And off he went, running up and down the gymnasium floor, stickhandling the ball like a pro. He was quick and nimble and he could deke and fake out other players with a shimmy and a shake of his head. They thought he was going one way—and he went the other. Into the net the ball went.

"Goal!"

He scored goal after goal after goal, drunk on the success of scoring at will. His thirst for glory was finally fulfilled.

At the end of the game, exhausted and sweaty, he looked up for Trish's admiration. But she was gone. He asked the other kids, "Where did Trish go?" He said quietly to himself, "Where did she go?"

One of the other girls said, "She got bored and left *hours* ago!"

At that moment our boy realized: if having a woman meant having to give up hockey, then he would stay happily single. Women weren't for him. At least not yet.

4

Takin' Care of Business

The following weekend, the boy walked down the road to the fence by the golf course, beyond the creek, where the frogs and the tadpoles lived.

It was a beautiful, sunny day. He took his place up like he did every Saturday, by the hedge across the street. The boy waited for the golfers to mis-hit their ball over the fence.

He'd scramble after the ball, finding it deep in a holly bush, or in the hedge. Or better yet—catch it while it bounced down the road.

Then he'd run back to the fence next to the golf course and sell the ball back to the golfers. "Hey mister! You want your ball back? It's gonna cost you 25 cents!"

If it was a new ball, the boy would ask for 50 cents.

Most of the golfers laughed and appreciated his entrepreneurial spirit. The ones that didn't, never got their ball back. So he'd make a few dollars every Saturday and then went down to buy hamburgers and chips, root beer and chocolate bars.

His mom wondered why he was never hungry on Saturdays.

5

Independence Day

One day, he got mad at his mom and might have even sworn. His mom was upset and demanded an apology.

Feeling stubborn, the boy said, "I'm not apologizing. In fact, I'm moving out!" After all, he knew how to make his own money.

So he began to gather his belongings, starting with his coat.

His mother said, "What are you doing?"

"I'm getting my coat."

"That's not your coat, it's *my* coat. I bought that for you. You can put that down."

"Fine!" retorted the boy. "I'm just gonna get an apple."

"Oh no," said the mother. "Those are my apples. You

wanna leave home, you leave with the clothes on your back."

"Fine!" He said. "One day I'm gonna run the country and you'll remember that I started with nothing!"

His mother laughed "If you want to run the country, you'll have to do that from Wall Street. Money runs the world. Not politicians."

The boy thought about this as he left the house. *Money*, he thought. *That's how he'd build his empire.*

The boy marched down the street until he reached the hedge where the golf balls were. He suddenly remembered there was a big rock in the hedge. He climbed in and laid on the rock. *This is my new home!*

He felt proud that he had made it on his own in the world.

As the sun began to set, the temperature dropped, and it started to get cold. The wind picked up, and the boy was sure he heard something further down in the hedge. He thought, *Maybe somebody else is living here.* " Or maybe it's a *mountain lion!"*

I better go home, he thought. My mom probably misses me. Besides, I have to go to the bathroom.

The boy started to walk home, in the dark, one step ahead of the mountain lion. He *really* had to go to the bathroom. *Number Two!*

Now he realized he might not make it. And he couldn't believe it when he pooped his pants.

He was so embarrassed. He'd made a mess of trying to

move out.

Literally.

He knocked on his mother's back door. When she answered it, he said, "I'm sorry, Mom! Can I come home now?"

She gave him a hug and smelled him. "Straight to the bathtub with you, you stinky homeless boy!"

Maybe she was right. *His empire needed some work.*

6

Iron Man

Now that he had moved back home, he could concentrate on sports again. Road hockey, floor hockey, baseball… play fights after school. And of course, teasing the girls.

The boy loved his life.

He spent the next two years having fun. The only problem he had was eating an apple. His baby teeth never fell out, and so his permanent teeth came in crooked; in all sorts of directions. His front tooth was sideways. And when he tried to bite an apple, only one tooth would scrape a trench into the apple. Then he'd just throw the apple away.

His mother told him of this new thing called "orthodontists". She believed that they might be able to straighten his teeth. She booked an appointment and drove him there.

The orthodontist had one look in his mouth, and said,

"We'll be better off just pulling out *all* his teeth." Then he added, "Or, at a minimum, we would have to pull eight teeth out, and then he will have to wear braces, for at least five years."

What a choice!

The boy's mother said, "You are not pulling all his teeth out, he is only nine years old. Get him fitted for braces."

The boy was nervous. This sounded like torture! He said to the orthodontist and his mom, "I don't like apples that much anyway!"

They laughed and scheduled the appointment to get his eight teeth pulled out and his braces put on.

Two weeks later he was sitting in the dentist chair with his mouth wide open, like a baby bird waiting for a worm.

The dentist brought out a massive needle and said, "This is gonna hurt."

As if the boy did not already know that!

The boy gripped the armrest of the chair, squinted his eyes, and waited for his gums to be pierced.

The pain was fierce and shocking. He kicked and tried to be brave. Soon, his whole mouth felt frozen.

The dentist pulled out his pliers. Like a mad miner digging for gold, he wrenched them to the back molars and started to wiggle and pull.

The boy couldn't believe the orthodontist would be able to pull his teeth out, but sure enough, *Crack!*

The orthodontist pulled one out. The boy's eyes opened as wide as can be, and looked up the nostrils of the sadist who looked indifferent to his pain.

Soon the sadist grabbed another tooth, and as he was yanking on it, he said to his assistant, "I had a great fishing trip this weekend. I caught a fifteen pound trout! When I got him to the boat I couldn't get the hook out. I needed to use my dentist pliers to wiggle the hook free."

Just then he popped another tooth out. The boy couldn't believe it! Talking about a fish on a hook while he was working on his mouth. *This asshole was so unprofessional!*

The boy started to swear at him, but all that came out was a garbled mess of sound. "Arrrooouugg nasss ollllleee!"

Unable to stop him, the boy realized his only escape was to kill the dentist. Of course, he knew he couldn't do that—his mom would get mad.

***

After surgery, the boy was back home with frozen peas on his face, as he lay on his couch in front of the TV. Then, something magical happened: his mother gave him some pills that the dentist had prescribed. He took them, and soon had a feeling he had never felt before: all the pain disappeared. He sat with a swollen smile and stared at the television in utter bliss.

This was his first experience with being high, and he liked it.

7

Babe, I'm Gonna Leave You

One morning, the boy's father came into his bedroom. His father never did that.

The boy thought he might be in trouble, but it was worse than that.

"We're moving," his father said. Being a military man, he got posted to different bases in different towns, sometimes different countries, every two to four years. "We're going to Swift Current, Saskatchewan."

The boy didn't swear out loud. But in his head he said, *Where the hell is that?*

Swift Current?

Where the hell is Swift Current?

He didn't want to leave Vancouver Island. It had been heaven: trees and beaches and good weather: not too cold in the winter. All his friends, his school, road hockey, ice hockey. The fence that he balanced on to walk across the park.

Would he have to leave this all behind? His favorite hamburger shop. His paper route. The golf balls. The hedge. The creek. The tadpoles. The birds. And even God?

He found all these things there, and knew he couldn't take them with him.

8

Cat's in the Cradle

All the goodbyes were said, all the tears were shed. Our boy rode next to his father in a fully loaded Toyota Corolla across the country, while his mom and his brother took a flight.

The boy was kind of excited about the trip. He thought he would get to know his father—he hadn't spent much time with him before. His father was still a mystery to him.

The boy recognized his father's rugged and potent scent, reminiscent of a wild animal, which contrasted sharply with his mother's softness. His father was bristly. His five o'clock shadow was rough. And his brush cut wasn't much softer. His piercing blue eyes resembled those of a predator in the wild. The boy was scared of his father. He knew his father could kill him if he wanted to.

He remembered the time he stepped on a hornet's nest while he was looking for golf balls.. No matter how fast he ran, he couldn't escape the stings. This is how he felt with his father.

When he asked his father a question, he would ponder upon it, long and hard, as he tried to make it sound worthy of his father's attention. He endeavored to ask smart questions. Maybe even ones that would make his father smile.

He desperately yearned for his father's approval. He was still under the belief that his father could satisfy his thirst for love.

The traffic was clearing out as they headed out of Vancouver, and the trees started to whistle by as the road climbed into the mountains.

His father responded with one-word answers, never curious of the boy's comments. After a while, he switched on the radio. He said, "I'm gonna listen to this game," as the announcer called out balls and strikes.

The boy sank back into his seat and stared out the window.

Whenever our boy tried to show his dad that he had interesting things to say, and questions about things only men would know, his father would dismiss him and just say, "Go to sleep."

The boy looked out the window, and saw the trees and the mountains. He saw the rivers disappear. Then he got to the flat lands. Prairies. Miles and miles of wheat and dirt. No trees. No mountains. No streams to catch tadpoles.

This was a bleak land. A land for hard farmers and tough crops.

The boy's sensitivity would be tested in this environment.

By the time they reached Swift Current and stopped to get a sandwich in a Mr. Sub, the boy was beside himself. He was in a strange land. Nothing looked familiar. He felt alone and scared. *So alone.*

Where had his father taken him?

He began to cry. Uncontrollably. Sobbing, unable to eat. Just tears, and more tears.

His father became angry. "You're embarrassing me! What's wrong with you, smarten up!"

Try as he might, our boy could not stop crying. So his father dragged him from the store back to the car, and off to the motel room, to wait for Mother.

Our boy hated Swift Current.

9

The Boys of Summer

The family rented an apartment until they could take possession of the modest house the father had bought. They would be in this apartment for three months. All summer. A dry, hot summer. A prairie summer, with crickets and dust, wind and heat. Nothing like the lush rainforest that the boy was used to.

He saw the kids down in the baseball field playing baseball and begged his parents to let him join. So they sent him down to play.

He didn't know anybody, so he asked the coach if he could play.

"Sure." the coach said, "Go take shortstop."

The boy took up his position at shortstop, and he knew this was how he'd fit in—*if* he played well.

The ball was hit his way, and he attacked it like a lion on

an antelope. His heart began to race, he knew that if he made an error, fitting in would be much harder. So he came up and threw that ball like a pro.

"Nice play!" said the coach.

The boy felt validated. Here, on this dusty ball field, he would find redemption. Belonging. He could make a home here.

Each day, the boy watched the clock, waiting for baseball to start. Nothing else mattered. When the summer storms came in, he begged God, "Don't let them cancel the game!"

The hail fell like cannonballs from the sky. The boy had never seen hail like this before.

Still, he rode his bike down to the baseball field and stood in the hail. "It's not that bad!" he screamed out to the other parents keeping their kids in their cars as the hail was denting their hoods. "Come on, you guys! Let's play!"

The validation from playing well was worth more than the pain of the hail bouncing off his skin.

They all looked at him like he was crazy. They drove off, unwilling to be pelted by hail to play baseball. To our boy, it was much more painful *not* to play; he needed the glory to survive.

He stood on the field as they all pulled away, asking God why he had forsaken him. He pedaled his bike back home, retreating into the darkness of his room.

10

Everybody's Talkin'

It was fall now and school was about to start. The boy wasn't happy about this. He was starting grade seven, and would have to meet all the new kids.

Arriving at his class, he couldn't believe how big the other boys were. They seemed to be men.

He found out that in the spring, when it was time to plant seeds in the fields, all these young men left school, year after year. They were held back and made to take the same school year over again. So, there were 16-year-olds in grade seven.

He, on the other hand, was still very much a boy. A boy with braces. He had so much metal in his mouth, he would set off a metal detector if he walked through it.

Not everybody had braces: it was a new thing. The kids were cruel. They called him "Tin Grin" and "Brace Face."

He tried not to smile, hoping they'd forget what his teeth looked like.

The girls all giggled when they thought about kissing him and said to one another, "If you kissed him you would have to go to a hospital!"

But he was cute, and he was the 'new boy,' so the girls were still interested. The boys, on the other hand, didn't like him.

They went to gym class and the boy was a good wrestler. He pinned one of the popular boys and all the other boys made fun of their friend, losing to this little new kid with the braces.

The gym teacher told them at the end of the class that they had mandatory showers.

Our boy was terrified. He had never showered with anyone before. He even thought, *this must be illegal!*

How could he get out of it?

But it was explained, "No shower, no next class."

So the boy took off his clothes, ever so slowly, facing the wall. When he took his underwear off he cupped his hands over his little penis, and walked into the shower.

There were eight different showers in one big room, and all the other boys were naked. Unafraid, they stood exposing themselves with no shame, as they were already fully developed young men. The boy felt so ashamed that he was still a little boy. He quickly washed, as the other young men laughed at him.

He dried off, got dressed, and headed to his next class.

Getting to class a little early, he started talking to some of the girls in the class. They were interested in the cute "new boy." It gave him a pinch of hope that he had a chance with the girls.

The others from gym began to enter the classroom and saw that the boy was talking to some girls. One of the boys from gym class jealousy barked out, "Why are you talking to him? He has no cock!"

All the girls giggled. The boy had never felt so much shame. He had no response. He just wanted to die on the spot.

11

Mother

Later that year, in the spring, when it was time to plant the seeds in the fields, all the young men left school again. Our boy was glad they were gone, but he still wasn't brave enough to talk to the girls.

Instead, he joined the football team and got ready for baseball and hockey. Sports—that's where he belonged.

He made new friends and started to get comfortable in Swift Current. He and his brother shared the basement. His brother was in high school and didn't want his little brother around much, unless he was hungover and wanted him to fetch him some orange juice.

Their mother left their supper on the stove. She wasn't a very good cook, but she managed to put together a chili or a few frozen fish stick dinners, or some macaroni with hot dogs cut up in them. She always told the boys they should feel lucky that they always had a meal and a roof over their heads. That most people in the world didn't even have that.

She told them to be careful, because there were nefarious people in the world. People that wouldn't have their best interests at heart. She didn't have any friends. The boy knew she loved them, but she didn't like to show it. A hug once in a while, or a pat on the head. But she did instill in her children how to have a stiff upper lip. That if they wanted things in the world, they'd have to go out and get it themselves.

She always reminded them of the life she could have had, and how adventurous she was. But she gave all of that up because of them. "I'm sorry mom, we'll try to make you feel better," the boy said. "One day I'll buy you a new house and your own car - then you can go anywhere you want!"

The boy didn't know how to fix her. He developed a sense of needing to make her happy. But how?

The boys knew to stay downstairs when their father got home. They would gather their food and head to the basement. *Banished to the dungeon.*

The boy spent hours on the cement patio in the backyard, practicing his stick handling with a tennis ball and hockey stick. If he practiced enough, he could develop the skills that would be required to be selected on to the all-star teams, and make his way to the NHL. He imagined winning the Stanley Cup, the holy grail of sports in Canada, and bringing it home to show his parents, maybe *that* trophy would be big enough to get his father's approval.

12

The End Of The Innocence

Time marched on. The boy found himself in high school. He still had his braces. He was still good at sports. But not so good with girls. An older girl once kissed him and she put her tongue in his mouth. He pulled back, afraid she'd cut her tongue on his braces.

As he walked away from her he was confused. *Did all girls kiss this way?* He couldn't imagine why people would want to enter another person's mouth with their own tongue. It seemed so unsanitary.

This would delay his attraction to girls for a while longer.

He made a friend—Diesel, they called him. His real name was Dan, but he was as big as a truck, so they called him "Diesel". Diesel was on the boys' hockey and baseball team, and he lived just two streets down from the boy.

Many hours were spent together with Diesel. They

would play football in the snow. Some days, it was minus thirty and even colder with the windchill factor. Diesel was wearing his Saskatchewan Roughriders football jersey. Just the two boys, out in a field, full of snow and ice, tackling each other to stay warm. They laughed and loved the time they spent together. Not realizing it, it was the beginning of the end of their innocence.

Diesel was a gentle giant; a good-hearted, salt-of-the-earth Saskatchewan boy. His father was 400 pounds and could barely walk.

One day Diesel's father had a massive heart attack and died.

The boy was only twelve and didn't know anyone who had died before. He tried to console Diesel. But he really didn't know what to say.

Diesel's mother invited the boy to the funeral. She knew how close the boys were.

They drove in her station wagon down to the mortuary. They walked into the mortuary and immediately knew he should stay quiet. There were wooden seats and long curtains that adorned the walls. It felt like an empty church. The mortician gestured them forward towards the open casket. Diesel's mother paid her respects as she wept. Diesel went next, with a stoic look he held his emotions in check.

As the boy got close enough to see into the casket, he was very nervous as he had never seen a dead body before. His palms got sweaty and he didn't know what to think.

Approaching the casket, the boy anticipated seeing the large man. He peeked in and saw Diesel's father looking like a balloon with no air in it; his skin was off-color and waxy looking. He was small and had make-up on!

The combination of surprise and nerves startled a laugh out of the boy. Then another laugh. Uncontrollable giggling. He was so embarrassed, but he couldn't stop laughing. He was now laughing about laughing. He put his hand over his mouth, to pretend he was crying.

Diesel's mom glared at him—she wasn't fooled with his act.

Ashamed, he turned and ran out.

He made his way back to the car and waited for them. He felt so embarrassed. *Why did he laugh?* It was so disrespectful. He didn't *mean* to laugh, he was just nervous.

He hoped Diesel would forgive him. He knew Diesel's mother wouldn't.

She drove them home, but never said a word.

The boys went into Diesel's room. Diesel lay on his bed and took out his journal. As the boy looked over his shoulder, he saw Diesel wrote only one word that day: "FUCK."

13

The Good, the Bad, and the Ugly

At last, the boy felt a sense of belonging in Swift Current. He found camaraderie on his team and with the boys of the neighborhood. He had his best friend Diesel, and the Tremblay twins.

The twins had a home camera. The boys went out to the dirt cliffs with ketchup, play-guns and hats, as they filmed their very own Spaghetti Western.

The boy pretended to be *shot,* and dramatically fell off the cliff, landing in the soft sand below him, in a theatrical death roll. He hammed it up for the camera, dying with an arrow in his back and his face, bleeding ketchup.

The boy had many other friends. He really was part of the "gang." The boy's thirst for companionship and belonging had finally filled him.

The boy loved Swift Current. He could stay there forever.

But, one morning he awoke to his father sitting on the edge of his bed. That could only mean one thing...

14

Go Your Own Way

They were moving. *Again.*

A party was thrown for the boy at the Twins' house. They screened the movie they made. The boys laughed at how funny they looked up on the screen, but were proud that they had made their own movie.

Each of the boys tried to wish the boy well. It felt more like a funeral, as they all knew how far away he was moving, and that they may never see him again. After all, he was going to Toronto. Two thousand kilometers away.

It might as well have been the moon.

They all wished him well. They all knew he would be the only one leaving. They were all Saskatchewan boys, born and raised there. Most likely, they'd die there.

On the last day, the boy made his way around the neighborhood saying his goodbyes, saving Diesel for last.

Diesel was mad. He didn't want the boy to go.

"You know you're an asshole for leaving," Diesel said. "You're gonna hate Toronto. Who am I gonna play football with this winter?"

"Well, you still have the twins," the boy tried to console him.

"They're not you," grumbled Diesel. "You better come back, I mean it! You don't come back, I'm gonna come kick your ass."

They both knew Diesel was never leaving Swift Current.

The boy was sad. He knew he'd miss his friend. But he knew nothing he said would change anything. He would probably never see Diesel again. The friends he had on Vancouver Island were distant memories. Now, these friends from Swift Current would fade in the same way.

So he said goodbye to Diesel, like a soldier leaving behind his dying friend.

As the boy turned to leave, he said, "I'll miss you, buddy."

"Wait," Diesel said, and he gave the boy his favorite Saskatchewan Roughriders football jersey.

They didn't hug, or even shake hands. Their friendship was deeper than that. The boy just turned and walked away.

15

Hot Child In The City

The boy was about to go from a small town to the big city of Toronto, the nation's biggest city.

After the long drive across Canada's second biggest province, Ontario, they entered the city. There were tall buildings, buses, heavy traffic, and people everywhere. The boy had never been to a city before, at least not one he was going to have to live in. He had heard of the big city before, but never saw it up close…until now.

He glanced out the window, hoping to see someone who might want to play hockey this winter, ride bikes, or play football, but all he saw were people scurrying around, going somewhere, fast. They didn't look like they wanted to play.

Where would he find people who wanted to have fun? Where would he find his next Diesel, his next best friend? Where would he find his next group of friends? Where would he find his place of belonging? These questions and more flooded his mind as he watched the city bustle around him.

They moved into the house and it had a basement. The boy and his brother were told their bedrooms were downstairs. They went down to explore the space.

The basement had a small window, where only a little light could come in. It was an underground basement, so the window was at the very top of the wall. The basement had a carpet, but it was a thin carpet laid over top of cement. The boy felt like a groundhog, hidden from the world, but safe in his hole.

The boy's older brother wasn't home much, as he had gone off to university. So, the boy had the basement to himself most of the time. He liked his time alone. He had a TV and a couch, and he could eat on his own and watch TV. The boy made funny faces, and acted out the characters from his favorite shows. Quite often he talked to himself, sang songs, pretending he was the lead singer of a rock band. It was a real variety show, the boy was a hit.

He was sure to be discovered soon.

The boy didn't start school for another month, so he had time to explore the city. He got a bus pass and started to ride the city buses. He would leave the house in the morning with nowhere to go, so he would just ride the bus as far as it would go, and then get a transfer and ride the bus home.

He would ride the buses all day long, looking through the bus window at all kinds of people. Toronto was a diverse place; it had all kinds of cultures and ethnicities. He was shocked by all the different people, as he had never really seen anyone that didn't look like him before. But on these buses he saw African people with traditional clothing, they looked so colorful compared to the typical clothing other Canadians wore. There were Italian people who flew their flags in front of restaurants. The boy heard people speaking to each other in a different language, which he later learned was Lebanese. On the bus he also saw politicians and businesswomen in suits. He was fascinated with the variety of people.

But he did see what they had in common. They laughed and they had friends and they were all going somewhere.

He knew that none of them would care how good of a baseball player he was. He knew he would never be part of their lives. Just an observer, like a kid staring through the glass at a party going on outside.

Whenever the boy got on the bus he always made his way to the back, and hoped that the last seat was empty. He would take up his position in the back corner—just like his basement, he felt safe in the corner. From there, he watched all the people get on and off the buses, and he looked out the window at the changing scenery of the city, trying to memorize all the streets in case one day he was lost.

He'd ride the bus all day long, always catching the last bus of the day, to take him home. His mother would ask him "Where have you been all day?"

The boy would tell her of all the places he saw and all the adventures he had that day.

His mother thought it was such a clever idea to learn the city. She would never dare do something like that. She preferred the safety of staying home. Staying home in her sadness with the thoughts of the life she might have had.

16

Sharp Dressed Man

The boy wore braces for five long years. Elastic bands and metal pulled at his teeth, cutting the insides of his cheeks, so often that he wore wax on top of the braces, to protect his gums and cheeks. His teeth were always sore as they were constantly on the move.

The day had finally come when the boy had had enough, and didn't want braces anymore. He could see his teeth were straight enough.

So that day, in the orthodontist's chair, the boy told him to take them off.

The orthodontist said the boy needed a few more months. But no sale. "Close enough. Take them off!" He needed his smile to attract what he was after.

Begrudgingly, the orthodontist began to free the boy from five years of incarceration.

He removed the bands from the teeth that had been there for years. The smell was disgusting. It smelled like food that had been left out of the refrigerator on a hot summer's day.

But when he was finally free from all the metal, it felt as if he had no teeth in his mouth.

After rinsing with mouthwash and spitting, the boy glided his tongue from one molar, across the front of his teeth, to the rear molar. He couldn't believe how smooth his teeth felt. No longer would his tongue get caught in the metal…nor would anyone else's.

When the orthodontist held up the mirror, the boy shed a tear. His five year ordeal was over. He looked like a movie star. *He was a handsome dog.*

17

Fat Bottomed Girls

One hot summer day, the boy took the bus to a small beach on a lake. The boy sat on his towel and looked around.

He saw two girls around his age.

He thought they were cute.

The girls went swimming. So the boy went in after them. He kept his distance respectfully, but watched them as he swam out into the cool water. The boy was conscious of his hair: he had long, flowing brown hair. To avoid messing it up, he refrained from putting his head in the water.

He noticed the girls were mocking him, holding their heads above the water so that their hair–which was already wet-wouldn't touch the water as they swam, mocking the boy's awkward breaststroke, like a turtle swimming with his neck stuck out of the water. He was happy they noticed him, but embarrassed they had discovered his vain attempt at keeping his hair dry. So he got out of the lake, dried off, and went home.

The boy was still shy.

18

A Day in the Life

It was the first day of school. As our boy walked onto school property, he couldn't believe how many kids there were. He could see them all huddled together in different groups: there were the smokers, and the stoners, the geeks, and the jocks. And the pretty girls, and the mean girls.

He didn't know anybody. So he just made his way to the classroom. He went into the class, and found his seat at the back row, strategically positioned for maximum safety.

He started to watch the kids interact. He never got to know any of the kids. They didn't seem very interested in him. So, he threw himself into what was being taught in the classroom.

During English class, he was introduced to Shakespeare. It was the first time he ever heard any Shakespeare and he fell in love with the soliloquies. *Tomorrow, and tomorrow, and tomorrow, Creeps in this petty pace from day to day...*

"To be, or not to be: that is the question: Whether 'tis nobler in the mind to suffer the slings and arrows of outrageous fortune..."

He loved the sadness of this. The bleak description that life was a veil of tears.

These words sounded as sad as he felt. He memorized them like an anthem for his soul. It was the first time he realized that words could touch his heart; that the meaning could sink like a rock to the depths of his being.

19

Run Through The Jungle

One day in the hallway the boy heard another boy talking about the football team and the tryouts to make the team. So he headed toward the gym looking for the coaches, to see if he could play football.

The boy was still small for his age, but he was solidly built and he could run like a deer. He had the fire in his belly that drove him to belong and be noticed; to stand out, to be great. This was how he would attract friends. This was how he might get a girlfriend. It might even be the way to his fame and fortune.

Each day after class he raced down to the locker room to put on the pads and compete, to do battle on the field like gladiators pursuing glory in the colosseum.

He was one of the fastest runners, so the coach made him a wide receiver, and let him return punts. "We have a star in the making here!" said the coach.

The coach even put him on defense to cover the other receivers.

The boy never left the field.

After practice, he still never made any friends and hated taking showers with the other boys. The other boys didn't seem embarrassed to get naked. In fact, one boy, Ken Dell, would run in the shower and slide on his knees naked between all the other boys, screaming "Woohoo!" He had no fear, no shame. He did whatever he wanted without boundaries, oblivious to what anyone else thought of him.

The boy couldn't comprehend this kind of freedom.

Soon the season started. The boy played well, scoring touchdowns and running punts back for great gains.

Game after game, he was leading the team to victory.

The team had a few other stars. Ken Dell was a ferocious linebacker. At the bottom of the pile, Ken would bite the calves of the other team's players. He was an animal.

Ryan O'Reilly was a big, tough Irish boy, who would hit people like a Mack truck. He loved the violence, even when he had the ball he would initiate collisions with the other defenders. He wasn't there for fun, he was there to inflict pain.

The boy knew he wasn't as tough as the other guys, but he could run and catch, and he wasn't in it for the violence anyways, he was there for the glory. The glory that would make him whole, that would make him lovable, that would make his father notice him and make all his dreams come true.

20

Crush On You

The team never lost a game; in fact, it was never even close. They really were a special group of kids, led by a coach with a serious football mind. Some days the boy believed *he* wanted it more than they did.

The leaves had started to turn color, as the cold winter air of Toronto settled in from the north. The ground became harder and you could see your breath. Winter was coming to the great white north.

The boy loved this feeling. His breath came alive right in front of his face. He had visual proof that he lived in a harsh environment. This made him feel *tough*.

He remembered days like this in Swift Current, playing with Diesel in the icy field, when his frozen eyelashes would stick together and the snot from his nose would freeze on his lip. Toronto wasn't as cold, but it more than made up for that with wave after wave of snow. The boy was tasked with shoveling the driveway for his father, so his father could get to work. Some mornings the snow was taller than the boy was.

After finally getting the driveway clear, the snow plow would come by, cleaning the street, burying the front of the driveway…again. The boy would curse at the plow, as if it would make a difference; it never did. It was just another lesson for the boy: when you think the job is over, it never is.

There were some advantages to having that much snow. The roads would get packed, so dense with snow that even the snow plow couldn't take it down to the cement. Before the city could send around the salt trucks to melt the icy snow, the kids could slide on the roads with their Kodiak boots that had no tread. When the bus arrived at the bus stop, they would all hang on to the back bumper and squat down like a skier, tucked in a speed position. And when the bus took off, they all held on to see who could go the furthest. Sometimes they rode the bus for miles this way. They called it "bumper shining". Some of his friends from the football team, and even a couple of the cheerleaders, would do it on Saturdays.

One of these cheerleaders was named Lisa. She was beautiful. Bumper shining gave the boy a chance to spend some time with her. He would position himself next to her on the back bumper, and they'd laugh and scream as they slid down the road behind the bus together. When Lisa would let go, usually from fear, the boy would let go with her, not because he was afraid—just so they could stay together. He had taken a shine to Lisa that thrilled him much more than the bumper.

21

We Will Rock You

The school football team made it to the playoffs, undefeated. It was the semi-final game for the entire city and the boy's school, Brookwood, was playing the rival highschool, Glendale. They hadn't played each other yet that season. As they were both excellent teams, there was no way of predicting how the game would go.

The sun sank early in the winter sky. The stadium lights shone bright. There were close to a thousand people in the crowd, kids from both schools, parents—of course, not the boy's parents—cheerleaders, teachers, and even the local press.

Part way through the first half, the boy made a spectacular catch, then weaved his way through the defense to score the first touchdown of the game.

The crowd went wild.

As he jogged out of the endzone after the play was over, his teammates rushed around him and slapped him on the back, hooting and hollering. The boy felt like he finally belonged. *He was one of them.*

He even glanced over and saw the cheerleaders with their pom poms in the air. He saw Lisa and hoped she had fallen in love with him.

Now Glendale had the ball and they were marching down the field to score their touchdown, but the boy was defending. He anticipated the throw from the quarterback and he sprinted in front of their player and intercepted the ball, running the length of the field he scored his second touchdown.

The crowd went nuts. The boy's team was crazy with excitement and the cheerleaders bounced with joy. The boy's heart was full.

Now the game was nearing the end, and Glendale had tied the game. They were punting the ball as the boy was deep in his own endzone, waiting for the ball to come sailing through the night sky.

The boy was trying to focus on the ball between the stadium lights. He knew he must catch it, for if he dropped the ball it would be death for the team and shame for him. He focused like an eagle on its prey as the ball disappeared and reappeared in the night air. He centered underneath where he thought the ball was going to come down, opening his hands just as the ball was about to land, cradling it like a fireman catching a baby.

The boy had it now, he stepped one direction, pretending he was going to run to the left, then quickly ran to the right. He outran the entire team as he sprinted down the sidelines right in front of the cheerleaders. He could feel the defenders chasing him. The boy knew not to make a misstep, not even to look back for that would slow him down and they would catch him. High-stepping, his knees were like pistons, as his feet pushed the earth away beneath him as he ran and ran into the endzone to score the winning touchdown.

The crowd erupted. The boy's team piled on him. He felt the praise from his teammates, the respect of his coach, the thrill of the crowd, the adoration of the cheerleaders, and the love of Lisa.

22

We Are The Champions

That week in school, he was the hero. But they all knew the big game—the city's Championship—was yet to come.

They announced his plays on the PA system in Home Group, the first class in the morning and reminded everybody in the whole school to attend the championship game the following Saturday night.

In his school there were three thousand students, and all of them would be there Saturday night.

Brookwood had never won the city championship before and it was a big deal. The pro scouts would be there, the game would be televised, and many of the best players would get drafted and receive scholarships to play football in university. This was the route to get to the pros.

The boy tried to be humble all week, attempting to not let the pride he felt show through. He saw Lisa, standing at her locker and he summoned the courage to go talk to her. He asked her out on a date and she said "yes."

After all, he was the man of the hour.

At home, the boy told his parents about how well he'd played. His mom was supportive but not that interested. Yet his father listened. He seemed curious: was this boy of his really going to be able to follow in his footsteps? Was he a great athlete? Maybe even make the pros?

The boy could see he had his father's attention, maybe for the first time in his life.

23

Love Is Like Oxygen

The big date night came and the boy walked down to Lisa's place, who lived less than a mile away.

He had his Kodiak boots on, blue jeans, a white T-shirt and a jean jacket—a "Canadian Tuxedo." He felt like a million bucks.

He knocked on her door, and was hoping her father wouldn't answer. As the door swung open he saw a vision of loveliness: Lisa had her hair just right, and a pretty flower dress on, he could see the curve of her body and her long legs.

Her eyes shone like the sun.

They made their way down to the bus stop and caught the bus to the mall. This time they rode inside the bus.

The boy didn't know what movie to take her to, so he just bought two tickets to whatever was playing. It was some obscure movie with no famous stars, something about a boxer named Rocky.

As he sat in the darkness he was strangely compelled by this movie, and he summoned up the courage of that boxer to reach out in the darkness to touch her hand.

His heart raced as Lisa's fingers interlaced, embracing his hand into hers. It felt better than anything he had experienced in his life.

She liked him. She was his girl.

On the way back, they stopped a block from her house. He wanted to kiss her, but she was a good six inches taller than him. So he stood on the curb, to look her in the eye and had a change of heart. He didn't want to embarrass her, she was a good girl, and he did not want to go too fast.

So he delivered her to her doorstep, and said good night.

Mission accomplished.

His heart raced as he floated back home.

24

Dreamer

That night, the boy laid in bed dreaming about the upcoming championship game. The scouts, the cameras, and the cheerleaders—especially Lisa—and maybe even his Dad, all watching him perform like he had the week before.

He imagined getting a scholarship, going to university, and being a star. Then, on to the pros, to live a great life with Lisa and all their kids. To have money and fame and win at the game of life. The game on Saturday seemed like Christmas coming, the beginning of his life, not anything he should worry about.

How could anything go wrong?

25

Armageddon

The day had arrived, Championship Saturday. The newspapers had written articles about the clash of the titans. Brookwood, the team that had never won the title, but was undefeated so far this year, and Charlebois, the French school who were perennial champions and a force to be reckoned with.

It was a sunny day, crisp and cold. It was just above freezing, late in November. The game was played at the city stadium, where the pros played, and the stands were filled with thousands of people. Camera crews were on the sidelines, newspaper reporters, television reporters and announcers and scouts from the pro teams were there.

For boys his age, this was the biggest showcase of talent possible. Our boy was ready.

He taped his ankles and wrists to make him stronger like he did every game and painted his face with black smudges to reflect the winter sun. His team knew victory was near, for they hadn't tasted defeat all year, and the boy was gonna take this team to a championship.

The coach gave a fiery speech, telling the team there was no tomorrow, but today was the most meaningful day of their lives, a day that would shape their destiny forever.

"Seize the moment. The spoils go to the victor. Glory is ours, men! Make it happen! It's up to you! Let's Gooo!"

As the game began, the boy's team could immediately sense this was a *different* opponent. The plays that they had made so easily all year were not working. The crowd could feel the team's frustration grow every time they failed to move the ball.

They managed to keep the other team within a touchdown, late into the fourth quarter, scoring only a field goal themselves. The other team was winning 7-3, with only a couple minutes left on the clock. They needed a touchdown. Another field goal would not suffice.

With only a couple minutes left, Charlebois was punting the ball to Brookwood for one last chance. The crowd was eerily quiet. The boy stood in his endzone, waiting again for that ball to sail through the night sky for him to catch. Just then, he looked across the field and saw his father standing at a fence, watching him.

He had never seen his father at one of his games before. The curiosity got his father off the couch and had him drive down that cold night to watch his son.

The boy imagined catching the ball, faking to the left, and running to the right, right down that sideline, right past his father as he scored the winning touchdown for the championship.

Time slowed down. It seemed the ball was suspended in mid-air. Distracted by his father, the boy ignored his coach who wanted him to let the ball roll through the endzone, because they would still keep the ball and go out to the forty yard line to start their drive for the touchdown they needed.

But the boy had visions of glory. He knew what he was capable of. He wanted to show his father what he had done last week. So he centered himself and caught the ball, stepped to the left, and then reversed to the right, unaware of the wall of Charlebois defenders.

He was hit—hit so hard, the ball fell from his hands. The Charlebois players pounced on it, scoring a touchdown and ending any hope of Brookwood's comeback.

It was over.

And it was all his fault.

As he stood up from the wreckage, he looked in only one direction: to where his father had been standing at the fence. All the boy could see was his father's back walking away.

26

Behind Blue Eyes

As the game ended the boy's teammates grumbled to each other. Nobody would speak to him.

The boy sat on the bench with his helmet off and his head in his hands, broken, with no one to console him.

He could hear his coach swearing. "He lost us the whole game trying to be a hero!"

The team made its way to the locker room and the boy stayed on the bench. He wanted everyone to leave before he went into the dressing room. After some time, he made his way in to take off his equipment.

He saw a bottle of vodka on the bench amongst some bottles of champagne and cans of beer that were meant for the afterparty, he put it inside his bag.

He stood in the shower and tried to wash away the shame but it was on the inside of him. He could clean his skin, but he had no idea how he was going to clean his heart.

He got dressed and went out into the dark night.

The stadium lights had been turned off. The crowd was gone, the cameras were gone, the scouts were gone. His dream was gone.

He went outside and sat down on the cold ground under the bleachers and cracked open that bottle of vodka. He had a hole in his stomach, a hole so big he could feel the wind blow through it. He felt the sacred pain, a pain of loneliness, the pain of self loathing.

He didn't deserve to live.

He tipped the bottle up, and drank that vodka into the abyss of his soul, hoping somehow it would ease the pain and fill it. This was his solution to life now, this would be his answer to everything.

27

Comfortably Numb

That Monday at school, the boy showed up, but he wasn't there anymore—just an empty suit.

He was young and still lacked the ability to deal with life emotionally. He had no perspective on the ups and downs that occurred in everyone's life. This event felt like a life-ending tragedy. The boy was never taught how to lose with dignity.

He could hear his classmates talking to each other, but he could not hear what they were saying. It was like he was under water, trying to hear the voices on the surface.

The morning announcements had a different tone this Monday. The principal tried to console the school on its loss over the weekend, by congratulating the team for a great season.

But when he finished the announcements with "We

deserve better," the boy filled with shame again. His teammate sitting behind him jeered, "Good play, hero."

At lunch, he went to sit with all his friends on the football team, but nobody made room for him on the bench.

He made his way over to sit with the stoners; he knew they didn't give a shit about football. He wasn't ready to start getting high with them yet, but at least they didn't judge him.

28

One Bourbon, One Scotch, One Beer

That Friday night the boy talked his neighbor Bobby into going to the liquor store with him. Bobby was in his class too, but he was still friends with the boy, who was probably his only friend.

They were way under age, so they weren't going to get served at the liquor store but they both had money from their part time jobs. The boy stood at the side of the building, and as people got out of their cars to go into the liquor store he said, "Hey! Pick us up a case of beer, we'll give you ten bucks!"

The first few said no, yet the boy was persistent and he doubled down on his charm, one guy finally agreed. The guy gave them their case of beer, and they paid him ten dollars extra for it.

They headed down to the creek, under the overpass. Nobody was ever there, it was a little piece of nature in the city, and the bushes hid them from the cars above.

They sat on the rocks and started to drink the beer. After about three beers, they were already feeling drunk and full. He forced down another one, and then got dizzy, throwing up into the creek.

The boy felt embarrassed that he couldn't hold his liquor, but he drank a few more anyway. They were getting drunk now. When they climbed out from under the bridge, the boy felt free again, he finally felt like himself again. So he jumped up on the guardrail of the highway and unsteadily walked his way along the top of the railing. There was a huge drop down to the creek, but he didn't care. He felt like he was eight years old again, walking along the top of the fence back on Vancouver island. The alcohol was working, replacing his shame with confidence.

29

Run Like Hell

At school, the boy made his way around the lockers carefully, he didn't want to run into anyone from the team. He'd go from classroom to classroom quickly, as he didn't want to be caught in the hallway.

It first started with Ryan O'Reilly. He was the alpha on the football team, they used to be friends. Now, because of the fumble, Ryan had been given the green light to turn his violent nature towards the persecution of the boy.

Ryan cruised the hallways with a pack of hyenas, laughing at any stupid thing he would say.

One day, Ryan caught the boy alone by the lockers and decided to corner him. He towered above the boy and punched him in the head while all the other boys laughed.

The boy learned to peek around the corners and down hallways before he'd venture out into the open plain. If the coast was clear, he'd run from classroom to classroom.

After school he was targeted too.

In the mall, arcades were the gathering places of the young gamers who saved their quarters to go play Pacman or Galactica, or to emulate Pete Townshend and chase the Pinball Wizard.

One evening, the boy was leaving the mall, when suddenly he was trapped between the store and the bus stop. Then, he spotted Ryan O'Reilly with the boy's neighbor, Bobby.

The boy thought he might be safe with Bobby there, but Ryan approached him and punched him in the face anyway. The boy did not fight back, because Ryan was twice his size.

During the assault, the boy noticed Bobby was laughing. This hurt more than the punches—even his only friend was scared to stand up to the wrath of O'Reilly.

He was bound and determined to create some armor, a shield against anyone or anything that could break his heart or crush his spirit again.

30

Love Hurts

The football team was having an after-season party, and the boy had mixed feelings. He wanted to go so he could see Lisa, because he knew that she'd be there, but he had to find out beforehand if Ryan O'Reilly was going.

He heard through the grapevine that O'Reilly was out of town. So, delighted with the opportunity to go have some fun, and see if he could talk to Lisa, the boy headed over to the party.

As he entered the house, Carl Jones, the other alpha on the team, was standing with a mic at the front of the room, singing.

Everybody was dancing and some guys were on the couch smoking hash as the boy got himself a beer. His eyes scanned the room for Lisa but he couldn't see her.

As he walked down the hallway looking for the

bathroom, he opened a door to Hell. Ken Dell was kneeling on the bed, with some girl giving him head. Dell yelled at him, "Get the fuck outta here!"

The boy, surprised and embarrassed, was about to turn and leave when the girl turned her head, and the mystery was exposed.

It was Lisa!

The boy stood in shock, staring at her in disbelief. *How could it be Lisa? How could she be with Ken Dell, the crazy half-wit linebacker?*

She was so innocent! At least, that's what he had thought. *What a fool he was. He should've kissed her,* but seeing this, he would *never* want to kiss her again.

His entire fantasy of Lisa being the one for him, was smashed into a million pieces. *Were all women like this?*

His adolescent mind decided there and then that he needed to grow up. He needed to become more like Ken Dell: women must be conquered, not put on a pedestal. He would not make that mistake again.

That image stood still in his mind, as his perception of romance and love was obliterated. It was almost as if he could feel his heart harden. A fool for love would not be his folly. He would now see women as objects of pleasure, as sexual creatures, to seduce, satisfy and leave behind.

Determined to make this adjustment immediately, he went back out to the living room and decided to smoke hash with the boys on the couch. His mission to toughen himself up, to get rid of his childishness, was well on its way. "Let me try that," he said in a painful surrender of his innocence.

Somebody lit the bowl of hash for the boy. As he inhaled, the smoke traveled up through the bong, deep into his lungs. He coughed and coughed till his eyes watered. But when he lay back on the couch, the pain had eased.

He closed his eyes and felt peace and happiness. He wanted to keep it forever. That bliss…it was something he had never experienced since he took the drugs from the dentist. Now, he had found it again, and didn't want to let it go.

From that day forward he would be stoned every day.

31

Growing Up

That summer he was fifteen. A teenager to the core, he indulged in masterbating and smoking hash daily. He had a way to fund his new habit by working in a downtown restaurant, as a dishwasher.

At the restaurant he would learn many things, the first lesson was how to get thick skin. There was a chef named Dick Boudrieau who would say to the boy, "You are good and kind, good and kind." That's all that Dick would say to the boy. All night as he would scrub dishes and load the dishwasher: "Good and kind...good and kind."

The boy was proud of this job. He was learning how to earn money, and survive an eight hour shift in a kitchen. After a few weeks, when Dick decided he liked the boy, he finally gave him the punchline: "You are good and kind, good and kind: good for nothing and kinda stupid."

They all laughed hysterically. The boy laughed too. He

couldn't believe the patience that Dick had to drag that joke out for weeks. He was learning to be a man: *sometimes you had to be patient if you wanted the full effect.*

Dick didn't have many nice things to say about anyone, but he had a soft spot for the boy. One night a waiter came to the kitchen and said that a man in the dining room was complaining about how his steak was cooked, and that he wanted to "speak to the chef." Dick sent the boy out to the dining room.

The fifteen-year-old dishwasher stood at the man's table as he berated him on what a medium rare steak should look like. The boy smiled and said, "Looks okay to me." The man was furious.

The boy headed back to the kitchen as Dick was on the floor, laughing. The boy learned then: *you had to have fun, especially under pressure.*

The kitchen always closed at midnight, and every night just before midnight, the kitchen had been cleaned, floors mopped and everything put away, the phone would ring from the piano bar upstairs, the same drunk and nasty lady would put in her order. This infuriated Dick.

"I'll teach that bitch," Dick said. He took the soup out of the fridge and filled a bowl with it. Then, he undid his zipper, took his penis out and stirred the soup with it. He reheated it up and sent it upstairs. The report they got back was that it was "delicious." *The boy was learning a lot. Never piss off the person who is cooking your meal for you.*

One night Dick said he was taking the boy out for a drink. The boy was only fifteen, so they had to drive across the river, where the bars didn't care so much about age.

He took the boy into a loud nightclub. They sat at a table. The boy was handsome with curly hair and blue eyes, a strong chin and an athletic body.

Dick had told him that the women would be all over him. So he ordered the boy a drink and disappeared.

Soon men started to come to the table, and they were being very friendly with the boy, they were touching his hand, beaming at him, blinking their eyes, and the boy was confused. Until he looked up and realized that there were *only men* in this bar. Then he saw Dick laughing and pointing at him as the boy was surrounded by gay men. *Dick got him again!*

He came and rescued the boy and they left. The boy had a good sense of humor and wasn't mad at Dick. He admired his cunning.

Dick got cancer that year and died before Christmas.

32

Doctor Jimmy

The boy stayed on at *The Roast Beef House* as a new chef started in Dick's place. His name was Marcel. He was much younger than Dick and wore glasses, but he looked like superman. He was a weightlifter. The boy respected his strength.

One day Marcel showed him a way to get high at work. He took the gas canisters from the whip-cream maker and showed how they could inhale the gas, which gave them immediate head rush. "If you think this is good, you should try some LSD."

On Saturdays the boy would get extra hours vacuuming the piano bar. He'd vacuum all the spilled peanuts in the couches and chairs. He loved this part of the job, because there was a bar up there. He would get drunk taking shots of vodka and then wear it off while working.

He loved to pull the cushions out of the chairs and

couches and find all the spare change that had fallen out of the pockets of the drunken patrons from the night before. Sometimes he would even find hash.

The boy started to steal bottles from the bar and hide them in the kitchen. That night when he and Marcel were leaving, the boy had a bottle of vodka in each hand.

Marcel, knowing he could spook the boy, yelled, "Run! It's the cops!"

As the boy ran as fast as he could go, he crossed the dark parking lot, laughing nervously. He escaped between two cars, not seeing the metal single-chained-fence stretched across the curb.

His shin hit the chain at full speed. It sent him hurling through the air as he tumbled, head over heels, smashing the back of his head onto the curb. He held both bottles high in the air and yelled, "I saved them!" But it had cost him a concussion.

He had his priorities straight.

33

Purple Haze

He became quite good at rolling a joint. He would buy some Export rolling papers and a pack of cigarettes. He would take a piece of hash, heat it with a lighter until it expanded. Then he would break it up into small pieces while it was warm and pliable. Taking a cigarette, he would roll the open end back and forth between his fingers until the tobacco came out. Then he would mix together the tobacco and the hasheesh.

Taking out a rolling paper, he would place it on top of his hand, full of hash and tobacco, and then invert his hand so the hash and tobacco fell into the rolling paper. Then he would take the rolling paper by each of the four corners and enclose the hash inside, rolling the paper until the hash and tobacco were tightly wound. Then he would lick the adhesive on the rolling paper and roll the joint closed.

He'd twist the end that would be lit, and on the other end he would rip a small piece of cardboard from the cigarette pack, and place it in the open end of the joint, creating a strong support, and then fire it up and inhale the drug deep into his lungs.

The boy would hold his breath for as long as he could, maximizing the effect of the drug, and when he could hold it no longer he would exhale the leftover smoke.

The effect was almost immediate. He would smile as the rush of peace would blanket his brain. His lips would get dry and his pupils would dilate. The trees looked greener, and the music touched his soul. He loved being high.

He loved hasheesh. It had a beautiful sweet smell. It was smooth, not abrasive like marijuana—in those days it had a much higher THC content. It came from Afghanistan. There was blond hash and brown hash, but the ultimate was black Afghanistan Gold Seal hash. It came illegally from the fields of Afghanistan, across the Atlantic, up the St. Lawrence Seaway, to the soccer fields, bars, and school yards of the East Coast. It was everywhere.

To be an expert in hasheesh gave him street cred. It made him feel important. And when he was high, nothing else mattered. It made the lyrics of the songs he loved sound more emotional, allowing him to pretend he was the characters in the songs. It put him in touch with what seemed like the opposite place in his brain to sports. He was changing sides from left brain to right brain. He was tapping into his creativity. He was expanding his consciousness.

The body stone it created made life seem comical. He could see through the facades of the roles people played, finding himself positioned on the outside looking in.

From this day forward he would look at the world with the perception of someone that didn't fit in, choosing the path of escapism, instead of the road to his destiny. What the boy had yet to realize, was the price he would pay for this temporary euphoria, was knowing his real life was worth living.

34

Ramble On

The boy was proud of his new persona. He was no longer vulnerable to the failed dreams of life. Cynicism insulated him. He could mock life and its need for black-and-white stories. Who *really* were the winners and losers in life? He could play the fox who claimed the grapes he could not reach were sour anyway. He had found armor to hide his self-loathing.

After being drunk and high most of the summer, the boy wanted to take his new persona on the road. He wanted to go back to Swift Current to show off who he had become. He was not trying to recapture his youth, he wanted his new worldliness to impress the people in the place he had left as a boy.

So the boy asked his mother if he could ride the bus by himself back to Swift Current. After all, he had been riding buses in Toronto. The Greyhound back to Swift Current would take three days, but the bus driver would be there to chaperone.

His mother didn't object, she would have liked to do the same; to leave on a bus going somewhere far away. She escaped vicariously through the boy.

His father didn't even realize the boy was gone.

The bus left Toronto early in the evening. After he got his ticket, the boy didn't make eye contact with anybody. He didn't really want to know who he was sharing his bedroom with that night. He gave the bus driver the ticket and found a seat next to the window halfway down the aisle. He didn't want the back seat because he knew that was where the engine was, and he thought he might be able to get some sleep. He put his bag on the seat next to him to make it look like it was taken and looked out the window as the bus pulled out of the city.

A few hours later, somewhere north of Toronto, the bus stopped to pick up new passengers.

The boy was in a seat next to the window and leaned over to look down the aisle, to see who might be getting on. He saw a beautiful red-haired woman who looked like the movie star Ann-Margaret, in a tight T-shirt and jeans. As she approached his seat, he threw the bag off the seat next to him, beamed at her and gestured for her to sit with him.

So she did.

This trip just got much more interesting.

The boy's raging teenage hormones and his primal urge took over and finally quieted the coward within him. He also knew she was a stranger and that he might never see her again. So he summoned courage from somewhere deep in his balls and introduced himself. They started up a conversation about where she was going and where she was from, engaging in small talk late into the night. They liked each other, they made each other laugh. The boy was quite good at conversation and he was charming.

He got a pillow and invited her to get some sleep on his shoulder. She lay her head down, and they were quiet for a while, as the bus rumbled around the lake head in the dark Ontario Woods.

The boy whispered, "Are you asleep?"

"No," she said.

Then she moved the pillow to her shoulder and she said, "Now, you try and sleep on my shoulder for a bit."

So the boy did, but his heart began to race as she moved his hand to her lap. She clearly wanted to escalate their friendship to a romantic one. But on a *bus?* The boy wondered how that could be possible.

35

Night Moves

His heart started to pound through his chest as he anticipated their surrender. Ever so slowly, he inched his fingers up the inside of her thigh.

He glanced through the cracks of the seats. The bus was mostly empty and they were driving through the dark woods above Lake Superior. He made sure everyone else was sleeping. It had to be three o'clock in the morning, and the dull roar of the bus' engine helped hide the lovers' sounds.

Could they really get away with this?

He laid back to enjoy this newfound pleasure. This was as good as drugs. And even better than alcohol. Every cell in his body was plugged in. The rush of endorphins ran up and down his spine. He felt like a god.

The boy was certain the whole bus would wake up, and the bus driver would kick him off somewhere deep in the woods, but he didn't care. He was willing to pay whatever price he must.

In the darkness of the bus, while everybody slept, they made love, quietly and passionately.

They both held each other and moved rhythmically until they collapsed in satisfaction and basked in the bliss of the afterglow.

Our boy was now a man.

36

Mrs. Robinson

In the morning the bus stopped and they had breakfast together. She asked him if he needed any money.

The young man declined but he did think it was interesting that an older woman might be willing to pay him for an experience like that.

She told him he was wonderful, and that he had made her trip. The boy asked if he could contact her again, and she said no; it was better left as a memory for them both.

She paid for breakfast and left to catch a different bus back home. The young man did not even know her name, but he would never forget that ride.

For the first time in a long time, he was winning. He found a way to have sex without the effort of a relationship. This would be his new, favorite kind of sex. Nameless partners, with no intimacy.

37

Runnin' With The Devil

The young man would have things to tell Diesel and the boys about this trip. He reboarded the bus and continued on to Swift Current.

Upon arriving, Diesel was there to meet the bus. The two teenagers embraced, happy to see each other.

That night they went to a party. The young man wasn't interested in talking with Diesel. He saw beer at the party, and girls, and he got drunk and made passes at all of them.

Diesel was annoyed, and could see this was not the same boy that left town a year before. He was different. Darker. Seedier.

That week did not go as anyone would have wished, as the young man had made an ass of himself all week long. He was drunk most of the trip and didn't ever remember why he came. He found it boring and was happy to get on the bus to go back to Toronto. He thought he was older than everybody, a man of the world. It was time to leave his childhood friends behind. He said goodbye with no feeling, like he was dropping off a coat that didn't fit anymore.

Diesel was heartbroken. He didn't recognize his friend anymore. The boy that had left Swift Current a year earlier was only a distant memory. This new guy didn't want to play anymore. He was hellbent on sex, drugs, and rock'n'roll.

He wasn't selling his soul - he was giving it away.

38

Hellhound On My Trail

Back in Toronto, the young man started to run with a new crowd. His neighbor, Bobby, and other "stoners" from school, the Smith brothers, and his main drinking buddy, Patterson.

The Smith brothers were unique, because they already had moved out, and were on their own. The oldest brother was of age to even get his own apartment.

They all gave each other nicknames. The Smith brothers became *The Smitties*. Bobby became *The Beagle* because of how likable he was, and Patterson was *The Bear* due to his enormous size.

Our young man, no longer a boy, became *The Hound*. This suited his thirst for booze, drugs, and women. He was on the hunt, and he pursued these pleasures like a hound on a scent. *Hooowwwooond!*

39

Shooting Star

The following year the boy heard of another school, where hockey was the main attraction instead of football. Richmond High had a great men's hockey team, and the boy saw it as an opportunity to save face as he ran away. He told everybody he was leaving for hockey but he knew that he was running from the shame.

Richmond High would be a fresh start. The boy could create a whole new persona, with all the worldly pleasures imaginable. Drinking and drugging and chasing women would be at the forefront…and, when he had to, playing hockey.

On the very first day, between classes, he found his way to where the cool kids were, in the smoke pit. Usually he only smoked when he drank, but now he was going to smoke during the day.

Sometimes the kids had joints, getting high before class.

He was in grade 12 and didn't care if he made it through the year. He was bored with school.

He made the hockey team. He was a good skater and could find the net. He thought he had made some new friends.

One weekend the team was heading across the border into New York for a tournament. They piled into their motel rooms and the Hound produced a bunch of hash that he smuggled across the border. Some of the boys got stoned that night.

The next day they were eliminated from the tournament. Not a great showing.

Upon returning to school, The Hound was called into the coach's office. He was confronted with the story that he had smuggled hash through customs, and could have gotten them all into a lot of trouble.

The Hound was more concerned about who ratted on him and decided to quit the team there and then. To him, that was a noble thing to do as he didn't want to play with a bunch of rats.

Now, he had no reason to stay sober. He showed up to watch one of the hockey games drunk. When he went into the bathroom to take a piss, he turned around and missed the step down. Falling backwards, he cracked his head open in the urinal.

When a few guys found him he told them he'd been jumped. He didn't want to admit he was so drunk he fell into the urinal. They called an ambulance for him, as the cut was quite deep.

Off to the hospital again from another drunken episode.

The Hound thought he was funny when he told the nurse he didn't need any pain killers. He was already drunk. "Just go ahead and sew up that cut!"

His false image of a tough guy seemed to work on the nurse as she giggled and gave him eight stitches. The Hound got some perverse pleasure from hurting himself.

At least he felt alive.

40

Wicked Game

One Sunday, Patterson and the Hound had tickets to attend a football game. They drank an entire bottle of Southern Comfort on their way to the game.

They went into a bar at the stadium and the Hound spotted a table full of women. He bee-lined toward them. There were two girls his age, and one who was obviously their mother. He said, "Aren't you beautiful?"

The mother said, "Yes they are."

And the Hound said, "Oh no, I meant you." He had tasted the fine vintage of an older woman, and he wanted more.

The girls giggled as he asked out their mother. She said, "Are you sure?"

"Absolutely," said the Hound.

So she gave him her number. He put it in his pocket and bid them farewell as he went into the game with his friend.

Patterson and the Hound each had a bottle of whiskey, which they snuck into the stadium hidden down the front of their pants. They drank the whole thing during the game.

The Hound was mostly a beer drinker, so all this Southern Comfort and whiskey did not sit well. As he left the stadium he passed out, falling onto the sidewalk.

Patterson called him an ambulance and left. The Hound was taken to the hospital.

There they induced vomiting as he had given himself alcohol poisoning. It took several hours for him to recover before they released him.

He felt slightly embarrassed but blamed it on the Southern Comfort. *More like Northern Uncomfortable. He would never drink that again!*

The next week, the Hound called the older woman and took her for a date. He was sixteen and she was fifty. The sex was incredible. In the backseat of her car, he moved as if he had done it a thousand times. He felt confident and she loved it.

They dated for several weeks.

One night in her car at the drive-in she asked him to go with her to get some popcorn. The Hound was still nervous about public areas, he didn't like to be around people any more. Maybe he was worried Ryan O'Reilly might be in there. He had an unrealistic fear by now, that his nemesis would be waiting for him.

The older woman was offended and was certain that the Hound was embarrassed to be seen with her because of their age difference. He was too embarrassed to explain the truth, so she assumed she was right.

Later that night she broke up with him, and that was the last time he ever saw her.

The Hound knew there was no future for their relationship, anyway. Not because of her age, but because he knew that dating meant being in public.

He wanted to live in the shadows.

41

Dancing With Myself

The Hound received a promotion at *The Roast Beef House*, becoming a cook for the summer in the outdoor kitchen. This was a kitchen that only served things for the patio, so it was a pretty simple menu. He really was a glorified prep cook, making salads, cold soups, and sandwiches.

The best part about the job was the waitresses, especially the one named Sally, whom he took a liking to. She was older than him, in her early twenties, already in university. He still didn't even have his driver's license.

The Hound liked her. She had an air of sophistication. She was self assured. She had short hair and a pretty face. Wholesome. She had a beautiful smile. She wasn't skinny. She was full bodied. The Hound loved her body. He'd flirt with her when she came to get her order and she seemed to like him too.

One day, she invited him to her apartment after work.

She lived in an old wartime house, a three story building with five apartments in it, with an old wooden staircase and a wooden handrail. Up to the third floor, where Sally lived.

She had that kind of apartment that university girls have: everything was neat, and there was all sorts of interesting art on the wall. She seemed so organized to him, like she knew what she wanted out of life.

She poured them glasses of wine and asked the Hound to pick a music record so they could dance.

The Hound spotted a Springsteen album: *Greetings from Asbury Park*. It was Springsteen's first album, but the Hound knew every word. When he dropped the needle onto the record groove, the piano solo filled the room. The Hound started to sing to her. He was lost in the music. He wasn't a great dance partner, but the music compelled him.

She tried dancing with him but he was in rhythm with the music and didn't pay any attention to her. He was singing into his fake microphone like he was The Boss himself. The music touched the Hound deeply. His heart connected with the sadness of the music.

She changed the record after the first song, and put on something much lighter and easier to dance to. She tried to teach the Hound how to slow his feet down and dance with his upper body. He thought he was supposed to move his feet as fast as he could. He thought that's what made a good dancer.

She gave up on him dancing and took him by the hand into the bedroom. They started to kiss, and she took off her shirt. The Hound was electrified about this bare-breasted sophisticated woman.

The Hound made love much like he danced.

Fast and furious, he was showing off his athletic prowess. She tried to slow him down again and stopped him as she was about to blow his mind. She took him into the bathroom and turned on the shower, climbing into the tub.

She told him to stand under the shower and *pee* on her. She kneeled in front of him. The Hound could barely believe what she was asking, but he'd had enough beer and wine that fulfilling her request wasn't difficult. So he urinated on her breasts. Somehow this excited Sally. He really didn't understand it.

They finished the shower, went back to bed, and the Hound got to finish what he started. He was turned on by how worldly she was.

She praised his body and made him feel like a young stud.

This affair carried on for several weeks and the Hound was taking it much more seriously than Sally was.

He was falling in love.

The Hound started to imagine them together forever. One day he brought Sally flowers, and started to talk about what their plans were for after the summer.

"Oh dear," Sally said. "You can't take this too seriously. I really like you, but this is just a summer fling."

The Hound didn't understand that. He was sure she'd come around.

One day he climbed the old wooden staircase of her

apartment building. He got to her apartment, and there were flowers and chocolates outside the door.

He thought, *That's strange. I never bought those.*

He knocked on the door and she opened it. "Oh, are those for me?"

"I guess so," said the Hound. "But I didn't get them."

"Oh," she said, realizing her mistake. She took them in the apartment and he followed after her.

"Do you have another boyfriend?" asked the Hound.

Sally said, "Well. I am seeing several other guys."

The Hound was hurt as he imagined them all peeing on her.

His vision of their future was changed. This girl was not going to be his wife. He believed her now. He didn't really mean anything to her.

He left quickly, knowing he would never come back again. *Now he could move his feet as fast as he wanted to.*

42

Lucy In The Sky With Diamonds

Still hurting from Sally's rejection, the Hound decided he would get wasted. He needed an escape. The most powerful high he knew of was LSD.

He wanted to try it.

There was only one guy that he knew would have it…

Shtickhead.

Shtickhead would have some.

Shtickhead was his name and LSD was his game. He was given this name by all the other kids in school. He had done so much LSD that any intellectual capacity he might have had was long since burned to a crisp. Shtickhead never talked much, just produced LSD, got high, and acted like a

Schtickhead.

As the summer wound down, *The Roast Beef House* was having a year-end party. The Hound decided to bring Shtickhead—not for his social graces, but so that they could both get high on LSD.

The Hound went over to Shtickhead's house and down into his basement. Shtickhead had a whole sheet of LSD called purple microdot. He ripped off two pieces and gave one to the Hound.

As the Hound put it on his tongue, Shtickhead told him to *not* swallow it. "Just put it between your gum and your lip."

The Hound couldn't imagine this little piece of paper was gonna do much to get him high. *How wrong he was!*

They called a cab so they could go to the party.

By the time the cab showed up, the Hound was tripping. He had goosebumps and chills going up and down his spine. He felt like every cell in his body was plugged in to some current running through him. He felt vulnerable. He didn't have his wits about him. It was like he became a different creature, walking amongst humans, hoping not to be noticed.

He got into the back seat of the cab. Shtickhead got in the front.

The taxi driver asked Shtickhead for the address. He didn't know that Shtickhead didn't talk, so he asked him again. The Hound started laughing uncontrollably, knowing that Shtickhead wasn't going to reply, and realized it would be up to him to try and spit out the address.

But the Hound could barely talk either. Between the uncontrollable laughter and the magic running up and down his spine, he wasn't sure he was even speaking English.

The cab driver was beginning to grow irritated, as he couldn't get an answer from either lad.

The Hound fumbled through his pocket, where he had the address written down, but couldn't bring himself to say it. Instead, he stared blankly at the paper like a kid hiding under a blanket, hoping the world outside would go away. He handed the paper to the driver and kept laughing, as he couldn't help but wonder what the driver was thinking. *I wonder what's up with these two little freaks?*

They arrived at the party and piled out of the cab. Shtickhead paid the cab driver. The Hound could see people he recognized from work lounging around the patio and the pool. There were people going in and out of the house. Luckily, Sally was out of town and wouldn't be coming. There was music playing and people were dancing on this hot muggy day.

As Shtickhead and the hound walked into the backyard, there was fresh cut grass around the pool. The grass lay unraked all over the yard and as the Hound made his way towards the pool, he caught sight of Shtickhead from the corner of his eye, rolling around on the grass, like a dog that had just found a mud puddle.

The Hound said, "What are you doing, Shtickhead? They're going to kick us out!"

Wanting to hide, the Hound jumped into the pool and as his head emerged from the surface, he paused just below eye level, as his eyes scanned the jungle. He felt like Martin

Sheen in *Apocalypse Now*, coming out of the river.

To the Hound's surprise, nobody noticed them. Relieved, the Hound climbed out of the pool, borrowed a towel and dried himself off. He left Shtickhead in the backyard, making his way towards the house. Some of the other employees recognized the Hound, greeting him with a beer and a piece of chicken. The Hound was happy to have the beer, chugging it down in one gulp.

As he finished the beer, he glanced at the chicken in his hand and realized it was a bird. The chicken turned into a robin and started to flap its wings. The Hound threw it up in the air, screaming: "Fly! Be Free!"

Everybody looked at him, unimpressed. The Hound felt the distance between him and them, like they had seen him for the alien he was.

Out the door, down the driveway, the Hound escaped. Down to the end of the street the Hound ran. He stopped at a bus stop and stood there, watching as summer clouds rolled in, casting a dark shadow over the horizon. He did not know where to go or how he could possibly return to the party, as it seemed he had passed into another world.

He had slipped into the fourth dimension. He was trapped in that nothingness. Separated. He stood there, horrified, understanding his aloneness.

He didn't know how long he stood there for, but it began to rain. The Hound stood in the rain, getting soaked to the bone, shivering, wondering if he would be able to return to the land of the living but not knowing how. Trapped between the raindrops, he stood, frozen in time and space, alone…at peace. He wished he would never have to

join the human race again.

43

Who Are You

It was Labor Day Weekend and the lads decided to go see a double header: *Rocky Horror Picture Show* and *Quadrophenia*.

Rocky Horror Picture Show went first. The Hound was amazed. Half of the people were dressed as the characters and knew the lyrics to all the songs. They even stood up in the theater and danced and sang. This was awesome—even if the Hound thought it was a little too flamboyant for his taste.

He saw the fringe people. He liked them. He could relate to how they felt, but he knew he didn't fit in with them. They were too brave. They could show how they felt and who they were. The Hound knew, whoever he was, it was deep down inside him and he wasn't bringing it out.

Then, what he really came for, the second movie: *Quadrophenia*. This was *The Who* musical about a young man who struggled to deal with growing up. Full of violence and anger. This, the Hound *could* relate to. He felt himself a hooligan. He didn't know why he was angry and often took on the mood and temperament of characters from movies and songs. He liked the character who just couldn't seem to win and felt at home with the tragedy of it.

After the movies the lads headed over to Macguire's, the Irish bar downtown. The Hound was full of excitement and agitation. This bar was known to be very rowdy. The Hound loved that he could stand on the tables, dancing and yelling, as he poured beer onto his head.

The Hound turned into Pete Townshend, jumping off the table in a scissor kick and an around-the-world arm swing. He crashed into a table and, like usual, he crossed over the line.

He started to fight with the people he had just crashed into, and soon found himself out on the street, drunk and alone.

The Hound wandered around downtown, lost and lonely. He spotted a massage parlor, and in his youth and ignorance, thought he might find some love and affection. He had never thought of paying for sex, but his need for connection outweighed his shame.

He went in, with hopes that he might get some kind of comfort and warmth.

One of the massage ladies took him by the hand and said, "Come with me."

He went into the back room and she told him to take off his clothes and get under the sheet on the bed. Then she left the room and told him she would be right back.

When she came back in she told him, "You need to give me the money first."

He paid her with the last of his money that he was saving for dinner and a bus home.

She took the money and started to massage his legs.

He was trying to find connection, without the disappointment of pain and rejection. All of his experiences served as warnings to not give his heart away. He had learned that caring came at a cost he was unwilling to pay.

As she touched him, he reached to hold her and tried to kiss her.

She said, "No kissing!"

He laid back and let her finish.

He sat up, feeling slightly ashamed, and even more alone. He had bought pleasure. Not with just money, but with the price of his dignity.

44

Jungleland

The following weekend, the lads decided to go see Clarence Clemons play. He was the saxophone player for Bruce Springsteen's band. He was making some side money touring by himself.

The Hound talked his way down to the very front of the stage and was mesmerized by the big man's noise. The saxophone sparkled and shone like the sun. The place was rocking.

The Hound was drunk, and his ability to defend himself against his impulses was gone.

Clarence put his sax down on a stand, right in front of him, as the band took their break. The Hound knew just what he wanted to do.

With a quick glance over his shoulder to plan his exit, he grabbed the saxophone off the stage and ran for the door.

He was tackled by security just before he got out. They punched him and kicked him and got the saxophone back. Then, threw him out onto the curb.

He lay there, laughing and bleeding, pleased with his attempt to seize the prize.

Then he realized how stupid he was. He didn't even know how to play the saxophone. *What did he plan on doing with it? Keeping it like some souvenir from a war?* Maybe he thought the power of the sax and the bright light that shone from it could be his.

He knew he didn't have any left inside him.

45

Rebel Rebel

The Hound now was fully onboard the addiction train, at full speed. Whatever was beyond that didn't matter. He let the drugs consume him; every day was a new opportunity for him to get drunk or high.

That's all he really wanted out of life now.

Each day at school he would go to the smoke pit to find someone else who wanted to take off for the day, usually it was Patterson. Patterson had a driver's license now and was using his mother's car.

The Hound would say, "What day is it today, Patterson?"

And Patterson would say, "Wednesday."

And the Hound would say, "We haven't been drunk on a Wednesday for at least a week! Let's get the fuck out of here!" And off to the beer store they'd go.

They'd drive around Toronto drinking beer while listening to Nazareth.

Sometimes there was construction on the streets. The Hound liked stealing orange pylons and putting them in the back seat, so that when they would go to park in front of a bar, they would park right in front, putting the pylons around the car to make it look official.

They thought it was quite funny.

The Hound would go home drunk everyday.

One day his father came home early, and came downstairs. He saw the Hound sitting on the couch, eyes glazed, unbalanced and slurring his words.

His father looked at him with disgust. "Are you drunk?"

The Hound couldn't believe the irony. *His father was a hypocrite*, he thought. *He drank every day too.*

"You're a loser!" his father yelled. "You're gonna be a ditch digger." He raised his hand to threaten to slap him. "I should smack you around for this!"

Heartbroken and terrified, the Hound took away his father's power. "Don't worry," he said, "I'm moving out anyway."

This stunned his father into silence. "Go for it," he said and went back upstairs.

The Hound was only 16. That night he packed his bags. He didn't have much, just enough to fill an Adidas bag full of clothes and a toothbrush. Like a hobo on the highway, the Hound caught the next bus out of town. He had an idea on where he would be going but wasn't sure they'd take him in.

46

Into The Black

The Hound took the bus out to the edge of town, to the Smith brothers' apartment.

Smith let him move in as long as he promised to pay half the rent, and then he got him a job on the golf course. This was not "a golf course." It was *the* golf course: *The Toronto Golf Club*. A prestigious, private course.

The Hound was given the lofty task of raking the sand traps. He started off with just a rake, but soon was taught how to drive the little tractor. This tractor could drive right into the sand traps, and with the lever he could drop the rakes behind the small tractor, and drive around the sand trap until it was smooth and ready for the golfers.

He soon realized that everybody who worked there—from the fairway mower to the greens cutter to the superintendent—all liked to smoke black hash.

Through the connections that the Hound had made at the restaurant, he began to buy ten grams of hash, each one individually wrapped in saran wrap. He would sell eight of them on the golf course to the other workers, and then he would get enough money for that to pay for all ten grams, so he got two grams for free.

This was his business school.

As he drove the tractor in the early morning fog, his brain filled with black hasheesh, he could hear the swallows and the purple martins swooping around his head, eating mosquitoes as the sun began to rise.

The Hound loved those birds. He loved their purple feathers and the shape of their wings, and how quickly they could change direction and how fast they could fly.

They were his good friends.

Patricia The Stripper

One night the boys heard about a nightclub act across town, with a stripper named Mitzi, who could fire ping-pong balls out of her pussy.

The guys had to see this!

They let Patterson drive. That was the first mistake; Patterson was known to get drunk and blackout, as he drove like an idiot. One night on a ski trip he drove them right into a ditch through a stop sign. So tonight they warned him, "Don't get too drunk. You're driving!"

They headed across town and found the bar. It was pretty busy.

The Hound didn't like that.

But he wanted to see the ping pong balls fly and soon enough, out came Mitzi.

It was the strangest thing he'd ever seen: she put the ping pong balls inside herself, and shot them across the room. Some of them landed in the pints of beer the wild-eyed men were holding.

Each time a ball found its mark into the pint, the crowd would go wild, like she just scored the winning three pointer in an NBA final.

The lads got drunk and soon it was time to head home. They drove back across town, and Patterson ran a red light.

SMASH!

48

Life In The Fast Lane

The window shattered and the glass flew in a million pieces like shrapnel exploding in the trenches of the Somme. The metal screeched and bent as the car was crushed and rocked back and forth.

They had been T-boned.

The hissing of the engines, screeching of brakes and breaking of glass all became still. The Hound couldn't hear anything, just a buzzing in his ears. He was concussed, again.

From a distance, sirens began to wail louder and louder as they approached the scene of the accident.

The Hound could hear muffled voices trying to get everybody out of the cars.

He felt lucky to still be alive.

Crawling out of the wreckage, and staggering over to the

other car, the Hound could see through the broken window, a dead man: he had a million pieces of glass lodged into his face, as he lay lifeless in his seat.

The Hound climbed into the ambulance on his own power, and they all went to the hospital to get checked.

This was the Hound's third concussion in only a couple of months. But the booze prevented him from feeling its effects. So off he went, ready for the next adventure.

***

The fourth concussion came on the ice that winter as the Hound was trying out for the junior A Hockey team. He had left school so he thought he might try out for the NHL. He crossed the blue line, made a move from left to right, and was blindsided by an opposing defenseman.

He was told later that he had hit the ice with tremendous force, directly on the back of his head as his helmet was blown off in the collision.

He woke up the next day, and had no idea where he had been. He now knew for certain he was never gonna make the NHL.

So drinking and drugging would be his big league.

49

Kung Fu Fighting

One Friday night, Patterson, Bobby, one of the Smith brothers and the Hound decided to go drinking across town. It was early afternoon, so the bars weren't open yet. So instead, they settled on getting some food at a Chinese restaurant.

The lads ordered food and started drinking gimlets, which were a combination of gin and lime juice. The Hound perfected a technique in which he could pinch the long stem of the glass with his thumb and finger and drink the whole gimlet in one twist.

He thought this was cool.

Ten or twelve gimlets later, the boys were laughing uncontrollably. The food came, and they feasted. This was going to be quite a bill.

The Hound, devilishly grinned and whispered, "Let's do

a dine-and-dash!"

Patterson and Smith agreed. Bobby did not. "No way," Bobby said. "I'm paying my bill and taking a bus home. You guys are on your own."

They laughed at Bobby. "What a chicken shit! Get out of here, Bobby. Pay up and go home, you little bitch!"

The Hound drank two or three more gimlets.

They were so drunk that they didn't even realize the entire kitchen staff were watching them. They'd been in the restaurant a couple hours, and they weren't very subtle. In the hours they had been in the restaurant, it had snowed a foot outside.

Throwing back his chair, the Hound yelled, "Let's roll!"

They ran out the front door and they could hear the kitchen staff on their heels. They scattered: Patterson left, Smith right, and the Hound took a sharp turn uphill.

The Hound's boots were heavy in the snow. He clumsily fell face first. He got up quickly, noticing six or seven kitchen staff with knives closing in on him. He scrambled around a car. They were on the opposite side of the car, and he stopped. He started to go the other direction and all six of the kitchen staff chased him in the same direction.

The Hound started to laugh as he realized they should have split up. He stopped and went the other direction and all six of them stopped and went the opposite direction again. This was too funny for the Hound. Here he was, a drunken thief, and he was judging the strategy of those that were chasing him.

He fell to the ground, laughing.

The kitchen staff pounced on him, holding their knives to him, dragging him back to the restaurant. Soon the police arrived, handcuffing the Hound and putting him in the back of the police car.

Go directly to jail. Do not pass go.

The Hound did not have a get-out-of-jail-free card. The police booked him and put him in a standing cell. It was a four-by-four foot-cell with a steel door and a small window with metal bars.

The Hound, still drunk, forgot where he was, or why he was there and asked the policeman, "Hey man, can I borrow a cigarette?"

The policeman ignored him.

"I'll give it back to you when I'm done!" the Hound laughed.

He tried again. "Come on man, give me a cigarette!"

The big policeman was not impressed. So the Hound quickly switched his tactic: "Fuck you then, you fat bastard!"

The Hound wouldn't get a cigarette that night—or any water. He slumped in the corner, cursing Bobby for being such a coward. *Bobby should have been there with him!*

The Hound wasn't in any frame of mind to look in the mirror and see that he got himself into this mess. He passed this blame onto others. He blamed Bobby for walking away from it all. He blamed the kitchen staff for chasing him down. Whoever or whatever he could blame to prevent himself from looking at his self-destructive nature. Only an alcoholic can lay in a ditch and look down on other people.

In the morning, Bobby came to the jail and bailed the Hound out. It cost Bobby the price of the bill to release the Hound, so the Hound decided he'd let him off the hook this time.

50

Sympathy For The Devil

The Hound liked to party but not in public. He and his friends would invade one of their parents' homes while they were out of town, load up on drugs and alcohol, then get wasted.

This weekend it was in Patterson's house. Cases of beer and some LSD were on the menu tonight. As the Hound and Patterson were getting drunk, they each took a hit of purple microdot LSD.

As they were trying to play a game of Monopoly, the LSD started to take effect. The dice left the Hound's hand in slow motion. Tumbling towards the board, it left a trace of many die across the air. It looked like ten dice in motion as it hit the board.

On TV there was a show playing. In 1978 the TVs were inlaid into huge wooden consoles. They were main features of furniture in the living room, heavily entrenched on the shag rug. The Hound watched the television for a moment and, shockingly, all the characters started to say their lines *toward* him. This freaked him out. *How could the characters in the television be talking to him?*

Was he glimpsing behind the curtain? Was he getting to see a new reality? Were the characters of shows always aware of the viewers?

The Hound called out to Patterson. "Dude! Come here! The people on the TV are talking to me!"

Patterson had wandered somewhere else in the house on his own trip and didn't respond.

The Hound got up and ran to the bathroom to hide from the people on the TV. He glanced in the mirror. His pupils were gigantic and he had shivers running up and down his spine. His zits looked massive and his nose began to form a hook. He looked like Satan.

He thought to himself, *I am Satan! Now it all makes sense! I am a fallen angel in league with the devil!*

He looked down at his hands that held a cigarette burnt down to the filter. His fingers were yellow with nicotine as he had smoked a pack in the last hour. He dropped the cigarette butt in the sink, and looked at the back of his hand which became a skeleton.

Aaaaaa! It was terrifying. Would he ever get his flesh back?

Just then the doorbell rang. The Hound thought it must be the grim reaper coming to take his soul.

It was only Bobby, bringing beer. Bobby would not do

LSD, so he thought he was bringing the *goods* and was proud of his case of beer. He had no idea Patterson and the Hound had traveled light years from a case of beer.

The Hound looked at Bobby as the song "Tommy" by The Who blasted out from the speakers. The Hound was annoyed at Bobby's interruption. He knew Bobby wouldn't understand the level of high he was walking into. He was deaf, dumb and blind, like the character in the song. The Hound screamed at him, "Get outta here! We're not all Tommies."

Bobby couldn't understand, he was in a different dimension. The Hound felt sorry for him—he would never have his consciousness expanded. The Hound's self image was starting to be cemented: he was starting to be good at being bad.

51

I Fought The Law

One weekend, Smith, Bobby, and Patterson went with the Hound to Montreal. They had tickets to see a Montreal Canadians hockey game at the Forum. They were smart enough to take the bus because no one was going to be able to drive.

On the bus, at the back, they each had twelve stubbies of *Labatt Blue*, 12-oz beer in short, fat bottles. They drank them all on the trip. The Hound was young and cheap, and decided to keep his empties. *After all, he could get 10 cents a bottle!*

After the game was over, the lads approached a bus for their return trip. The bus driver seemed to be waiting for them, and prevented them from getting on. "I'm sorry, boys," he said in a French-Canadian accent. "You cannot get on my bus. You are too drunk."

When his usual charm didn't change the bus driver's mind, the Hound switched his tactic to anger. "We're getting on the fucking bus and you can't stop us."

With this the Hound felt a hand on his shoulder. He knew it wasn't his friends as they were in front of him. *It must be somebody else*, he thought. *Somebody that was gonna get it.*

The Hound gripped his Adidas bag tight and spun around, smashing the man in the head with all the empty beer bottles as hard as he could.

The man flew backwards, landing on the floor. Just then the Hound noticed the uniform.

Damn.

It was a policeman.

Five other policemen tackled the Hound, beat him into submission, then took him to jail. Booking him in at the sergeant's desk. The Hound said, "I'll take the penthouse, preferably with a view."

52

Bad Company

Still standing in front of the desk sergeant, another man in handcuffs came crashing through the front door. Six policemen were trying to control him. He was a monster. Had to be six-five, 260 pounds, and he had a ski mask on. As the policemen wrestled him to the sergeant's desk he stood next to the Hound. The Hound was dwarfed by this hideous crazed-eyed giant.

The Hound looked at the sergeant and pleaded, "Please don't put him in my cell!"

Soon, he was in a cage with fifteen other men that all looked like murderers. There was nowhere to sit, only a hole in the center of the floor for a toilet. These animals shit and piss in front of everybody into that hole. *This was not a five star accommodation.*

Sitting in the back corner, he was worried about what his dad would think. *Maybe his dad was right*, the Hound thought.

Maybe he was destined to be a ditch digger.

His false pride came to the rescue. *Didn't they understand who he was? How great he was?* He felt different than the other men suffering the same fate as he knew he was better than this. The Hound knew he was a miscast villain. *Surely, he was destined for greatness!*

This would be a repeating cycle for him. A cynic's humor trying to make light of everything, using laughter as a shield. Then the ego kicks in to argue the case of greatness to the jury of his peers in his mind. Believing he was destined for greatness; the current circumstance was just a blip on the road to his destiny. Then the sadness would set in when he realized he was delusional. He didn't have the character to rise above this, and so he would drown himself in the bottle.

53

Telegram

The Hound was beginning to see only darkness in the tunnel, with no light ahead. There was only going to be more alcohol, drugs, depression, disappointments, and loneliness. He was a runaway train hurling himself through the darkness as he could not see how life was gonna work out. He felt doomed.

He was only seventeen.

Drinking was daily now. Each night, a case of beer, some hash, pass out, get up, go to work on the golf course, get high all day, go home, drink, and repeat.

The Hound would look around at everybody else working. He tried to think, *If I could be anything I wanted, what would I want to be?*

He didn't like manual labor. It looked like a tough way to earn a buck and he thought about different professional jobs, but he knew that he didn't have the discipline or the intelligence to become a doctor, a dentist, or a lawyer. This was part of his problem. He couldn't see himself doing anything: he certainly wasn't going to join the military or the police force; he didn't want to work in a retail store or an office building; he just couldn't imagine himself doing anything.

He hadn't talked to his parents in months. In fact, they had moved to another town. His father got transferred to another base, three hours away.

One day the phone rang. It was his father. "How you doin', boy?" He said.

"I'm good," the Hound lied.

His father said, "Well, I've gotten into something new. They're called computers. The military believes they're the future. You should come down, go back to college, get a degree in computer science. There's a community college here. They have a two-year program. If I let you move back in my basement, do you think you'd be interested in going back to school?"

This surprised the Hound, as his father was putting out an olive branch.

"Oh I don't know, Dad. I got a lot of stuff happening here," he lied.

So his dad said, "I'll send you a book on computer programming, see if it sparks your interest."

When the book arrived, the Hound flipped through it, then relegated it to prop up a crooked table. It looked like

Greek to him—something geeks would be interested in. Not cool enough for the Hound.

54

Ace of Spades

One Friday after work, all the guys from the golf course were playing poker. The beer started flowing and the Hound was winning.

Little did they know he was dealing off the bottom of the deck to himself. Every time it was his deal, he'd call kings and little-ones wild, and then shuffle the deck until a king was on the bottom. Then it was easy to drop himself that king as one of his cards.

With every pot he won, he drank more and more as his chip pile got bigger. He was drunk now and wanted to take his winnings and leave.

The other guys did not like this idea.

"You don't get to quit when you're up. We have to agree on a quitting time, so we can win back some money!"

"Fuck you." The Hound said. "I'm leaving."

One of the Smith brothers jumped out of his chair and attacked the Hound. They fought each other, chairs flew, tables flipped over, and soon everybody grabbed the Hound and threw him out.

That night, he realized Smith was gonna kick him out of the apartment.

Maybe those computers were pretty cool after all.

55

Bell Boy

The Hound woke up ready to accept his father's charity. At least it was a light at the end of the tunnel—he just hoped it wasn't a train.

When the Hound arrived at his parent's place, he was pleasantly surprised. It was a PMQ, private military quarters, but it actually was a nice house on the base. There was a staircase heading down into the basement. *He knew this was his place in the home. The Hound was a basement dog.*

He made his way to the basement, only to see a mattress on the floor and a small twelve inch black-and-white television. It wasn't grand, but it was his. A space he could be himself, while trying to attend college.

The Hound was offered a job washing pots and pans on the army base, a tough way to make seventy-five cents an hour. He was elbow deep in hot water for eight hours, scrubbing away mashed potatoes and burnt meatloaf off giant pots and pans.

That was the deal: his father would give him his basement, but he would have to pay for his own schooling. He had a little bit of money saved up from before, enough to pay his tuition, so the money would be his spending money. Money for books and food. French fries, gravy and curds—poutine—this was his main staple of nutrition at the college.

The Hound liked college. The classes weren't too long and there were girls *everywhere*.

So when he found out there were only four hours of classes per day, and lots of young people to drink with, he was excited about his life for the first time in a long time.

He took to playing Cribbage in the students' lounge. He loved this card game, and would play it for hours, as it was a good vantage point to check out all the pretty girls.

He spotted one right away. She had big hair, big eyes, and a curvy little body. Her name was Michelle. He smiled at her and called her over to his table.

She blushed and came over to see the Hound.

He was finally good looking: he had straight teeth, big blue eyes and curly hair, and an athlete's body. He asked her name and told her his, and got her to join the card game.

She didn't know how to play, so he said, "Come sit with me and be my partner." He took her wrist and gently pulled her onto his lap. She sat willingly, but she was shy.

Michelle would be his girlfriend for that first year, or at

least for a few more months.

It all ended when the Hound came back from a hockey trip and confessed he had slept with another girl. He didn't believe she would break up with him, but she did, so he learned to be silent.

The Hound knew then he would never be able to stay faithful. His appetite for women was insatiable.

If he wanted to play the field, he was going to have to learn how to keep his mouth shut.

56

(I Can't Get No) Satisfaction

The Hound was playing baseball one day at college, and there was a girl at shortstop, named Kim. She had short hair and too much make-up, with a rock-hard body and perfect tits. She had a big smile and was very flirtatious.

She zeroed in on the Hound and poured on the charm. The Hound couldn't believe how easy this was, he loved college.

That night he took Kim out, and drank his ten or twelve beers, and they hopped in bed. The Hound was fit, so he gave it to her rambunctiously for hours. It was one of his longest and best performances of his life. And when he finally finished, he looked down at her for approval, but she said with disappointment, "Awww? You're done already?"

He had never slept with someone more sex-crazed than himself before, but it would only take a few more sessions for him to realize that he was never going to satisfy a nymphomaniac. *This was* not *going to work for the Hound.* He needed approval, validation, not to feel like he didn't measure up or that he wasn't enough; he'd had that feeling his whole life.

How long would he have to chase validation through alcohol, drugs, and casual sex?

One day he spotted an older lady at college.

He'd had luck with them before.

Her name was Lori. She was only a few years older, not his typical attraction. She was plain faced, freckles, long brown hair, heavy set and small breasts. But when he mounted her she screamed with delight, she scratched his back with her long nails and had multiple orgasms. *This* was what the Hound needed.

He'd hang on to this one for a while.

The Hound knew he didn't love her, but it fulfilled his need for approval. Each time he could make a woman happy, he felt a little less sad.

He grew up with such a sad woman in the house and failed at making her happy. But now, in the bedroom, he could make women happy and this fulfilled a deep psychological need. The Hound realized that it was never going to work: no matter how many beers he drank, or how many drugs he took, or how many women he slept with—none of these were gonna fill the empty space in his soul.

57

Beast Of Burden

One Friday night the Hound was out at the bar. He asked a girl to dance. She had shoulder-length hair and a button nose. Pretty, but plain. She was well proportioned. Her name was Liz.

They exchanged numbers, and he called her later that week. He invited her over to his house and took her down to the basement. He had his case of beer and put on some music. Pink Floyd, *The Wall*. He was proud of his musical taste and wanted to share it with her.

He didn't wait 30 seconds and he was on top of her. Kissing her and pressing his manhood against her. He tried taking her pants off but she wouldn't let him.

He continued to try and seduce her but she told him it wasn't going to happen that night. The Hound backed off. *He would bide his time.*

It took another week or two, but he finally did it; she was ready, she couldn't resist his charms any longer.

The sex wasn't great but it was comfortable and it was obvious that she loved him immediately.

Soon the Hound was going to Liz's place every night. She lived with her parents and she had a basement bedroom as well. Her parents were good people, blue collar people. Her father worked in a factory, and her mother babysat other people's kids, so she was always making food. The Hound was there for dinner every night.

Liz's mom should have known better than to feed a stray dog.

58

The Thin Ice

The Hound bought a 100 dollar car, it was a light blue Honda Civic two-door Hatchback. It had 300,000 kilometers on it, and there was more rust than paint…but it started, stopped and steered; so the Hound loved it.

The Hound's father got him a job Friday nights at the curling rink, on the air force base. The curling rink had a small bar and lounge above the sheets of ice, so people could drink and watch the curling.

The Hound's job was just to serve the beers and drinks, then clean and lock up the place.

It was only the second Friday that he was working, when some of his friends came by. They were other base brats—kids with fathers in the military living on the base like the Hound did.

When the bar cleared out, it was just the Hound and his

buddies. They started to drink and finished all the beer in the fridge and cracked open bottles of vodka, and were down on the ice, as they threw the curling rocks.

They were sliding the rocks back and forth, drinking their vodka and laughing their asses off. They all knew they were going to get in trouble, but they didn't give a shit.

They left the place, unlocked, unclean with curling rocks everywhere.

The next day when the Hound's father came home, the war was on. His father leaned into him. "What the fuck is your problem? I get you a job on the base, and you humiliate me? Are you mental? Is there something *wrong* with your head?"

All the years that his father had ignored him, uninterested in any of his successes, but *now* deciding to be the judge, jury and executioner of his son's character. The Hound knew he had done wrong, but couldn't bear his father's scorn. He needed love, understanding, and connection.

Instead, he was buried in shame and the dam of emotions that were bottled up for years, broke free. Try as he might, the Hound could not hold back the tears.

Not wanting to show his vulnerability, he quickly covered it with rage. He was almost as big as his father now, but he didn't dare fight him. So the Hound just took his own sunglasses and crushed them in his hands and said, "Fuck you," as he ran out the door.

His father chased after him but the Hound was too quick as he scrambled into the Civic, locking the door. His father got to him a second too late as the Hound started the car up, putting it into reverse, and gave his father the finger, as he took off with tears streaming down his face.

59

Fast Car

As he sped off down the road the Hound was determined to never move home again and that night, he moved into Liz's place.

He knew he was going to have to pretend to make a more serious commitment but in his heart he knew he was still a womanizer. He would now have to be extremely devious.

One night he took another run at Kim, the nymphomaniac. She invited him to a staff party, not knowing about his relationship with Liz. The party was at the bar where she was a waitress.

The Hound drove his Honda Civic there and was drunk before he even arrived. Cheating was much easier if he had drunk himself past his conscience.

As the party went on, and the Hound became even

drunker, he tried to kiss another girl. When Kim's friends caught him, they were outraged at his lack of respect and offered to throw him out. The Hound found himself tumbling down the stairs into a snow-filled parking lot.

The Hound piled into his Honda Civic. It had snowed for several hours, and the roads were treacherous. He never planned on driving home and thought he would get a ride with Kim to her house and come back to his car in the morning. Now he found himself behind the wheel way too drunk to be driving on good roads, let alone through a snowstorm.

60

Wipeout

The little front wheel drive did okay in the snow, at least at slow speeds. But when the Hound pulled out onto the highway, and got up to full speed, he could feel the ice and snow beneath the wheels.

The snowflakes hit the windshield with such a fury that the wipers couldn't keep up with them. It was like trying to maneuver in a snowglobe.

The old car heater didn't work either, so the windows became foggy.

The Hound stumbled around under his seat to find the eight-track and plugged in *Steely Dan*. He started to sing and dance with the music.

CRASH!

Halfway home he lost control, and the little Honda pummeled into the ditch. The car was buried halfway up the door, and the Hound realized that he was stuck. As he tried to accelerate out of the ditch the tires spun ferociously.

"Shit!" said the Hound and passed out.

He was awakened to someone tapping on his window. He rolled down the window with a manual crank, and, not looking up to see who it was, he said, "Let's go get a sub, man, I'm starving!"

The policeman wasn't hungry.

61

Part Man, Part Monkey

The Hound went to jail.

Go directly to jail— Do not *pass go.*

"Call my lawyer! I've been railroaded! How do I get out of here? Hey, you, policeman! What time are you letting me out? I got shit to do. You look like a nice guy. Can I get something to eat? Or a cigarette? You like locking people up, don't ya? You fucking Nazi!"

Still fueled by the alcohol left in his system, he started climbing the bars of the cell like a monkey. He reached his arm through the bars, and tried to grab the police officer's hat. "Ooo Ooo, Aaa Aaa!" He was pretending he was a monkey in a zoo, but he was no monkey, he was just a loser in a drunk tank — a monkey had much more class.

This was his first drinking-while-driving charge. *It wouldn't be his last.*

62

Fool's Overture

The Hound made the College hockey team. He was very proud of this, as it was the one thing he seemed to do right. The team would ride the bus to other cities and the Hound would drink all the way home. He thought everybody was drinking, but usually it was just him.

He'd get drunk and sing and laugh and play-fight, and everybody put up with him. He was funny, and they liked the Hound.

One day he met a girl at college and invited her to go on the bus to watch a hockey game. It was a brazen act, considering he had just moved in with Liz.

She sat in the front seat with the Hound. He didn't even know her name. The Hound had no awareness of his effect on people and knew that he could get them to do things out of their character, but he didn't realize they did it because they cared about him. He would do things spontaneously, and seemed to only care in the moment, but everything seemed meaningless to him. Just a form of entertainment. Life was a barrel of monkeys to him.

No one on the team had ever invited a girl. The rest of the team started chanting: "Where's the Hound's girlfriend?" cause they all knew that he had a steady girlfriend—but this wasn't her.

The Hound couldn't believe that he wasn't cool for having brought a girl he didn't even know. He felt the moral judgment of his teammates and was surprised that they saw it as a *negative*. *Weren't all guys just interested in picking up girls?*

On the way home, the Hound ignored her, not wanting to feel more shame. He thought this was the right thing to do. He cared more about the judgment of his peers than about the feelings of the girl. Trying to appear to do the right thing, he distanced himself from her. She was just an object to him, and he could toss her away if she wasn't serving a purpose to him.

His moral compass had no magnetic pole. He tried to find self esteem. He validated himself by dehumanizing everyone else. He disconnected his conscience in order to get a rush of approval. Whether it was a kiss from a girl, or a laugh from a stranger, he needed to affect people, in order to feel his worth. He spent his day manipulating others to get a feeling of belonging. It was the only way he knew how to relate.

63

My Best Friend's Girl

One of his friends on the team's name was Bob. Bob had a very good-looking girlfriend named Lorraine. And the Hound wanted her. She was a beautiful girl, with big brown eyes, long brown hair and small perky tits. He could imagine them through her shirt and was besotted with the idea of him and her, like a crow spotting a shiny thing. The Hound couldn't help but think about snatching it up.

One day the three of them were watching *Conan The Barbarian* on TV. They couldn't believe how big Schwarzenegger was. Soon Bob had to leave, so the Hound stayed behind. He asked Lorraine if she was attracted to Schwarzenegger. "No, he looks like a freak," she said, "I like your shape."

The Hound made his move, they were on fire. He and Lorraine were instantly combustible. They gasped for oxygen as the flames took them higher.

She was a small town girl and admired the Hound's sophistication and he was smarter than most of the men she knew. She had fallen in love with him and he loved her for that.

Now the Hound was sleeping with Liz—who he lived with, Lorraine—when he could get Bob distracted, Sally—any time he called, Kim—when he was desperate, and anyone else he could pick up any given day...

And yet, it still wasn't enough.

64

Spaceship Superstar

In his last year of college, he had the system wired, the Hound had all the answers given to him before every test. He graduated with a perfect 4.0 average which we knew he didn't earn.

Some of the teachers would have given him that anyway, because he was on the hockey team and everybody loved hockey.

So, on paper, he looked like a prize.

Soon the companies started to visit the college. The Hound did several interviews and a company called *Country Packers* showed a lot of interest in him. They were looking for a salesman, and the Hound could charm the rattle off a snake.

They asked him if he was willing to relocate and the Hound imagined they meant shipping him back to the city, or somewhere close by.

Instead they handed him an airplane ticket, and told him the final interviews were a four-hour flight away, to the North Country.

He packed his bag and told Liz he was going far away for an interview, and that he would stay in touch. He pretended he was sad about it, but in his heart he couldn't wait for the adventure.

He cared for Liz deeply, as deeply as he could. But it wasn't deep enough to have a sincere promise. He wasn't really connected to people. Hiis heart had been encased in ice for some time now, and he had no intention of thawing it out. His humanity was but a fleeting memory. He had abandoned his faith, his belief in God, or his responsibility to treat anyone well.

Liz cried insufferably, and her mother warned him, "You'd better bring Liz with you soon—you two need to get married."

"Yes ma'am," the Hound deflected.

As he boarded the plane he started ordering drinks and lit up a cigarette, and looked out the window lost in thought, "I'm flying high now."

The Hound had arrived.

65

Telephone Line

The Hound arrived at his destination after a four hour flight, and staggered off the plane. He hailed a cab and went to his hotel. The loneliness sunk in already. A neatly-made bed, a small desk, green curtains covering a window that looked down on a parking lot. The electric heater made more noise than heat. He put his suitcase on the floor, laid on top of the bed, and stared at the fan, spinning nowhere.

The Hound thought of going down to the bar but knew it was empty. He needed human contact, and a bartender wasn't going to do the trick. Then he remembered an old friend of his father's had a daughter somewhere around here. She was about his age but he hadn't seen her since they were kids. He remembered her name and looked her up in the phone book. Sure enough, it was there.

He picked up the receiver and dialed "9" to get an outside line. When he heard the dial tone, he dialed in the rest of her number, waiting patiently for the finger holes to click back in place before dialing the next number. It rang twice, and then she answered, "Hello?"

"Hey, I don't know if you remember me. Our dads are friends, and we hung out together as kids."

She wracked her mind, and quickly remembered. "Of course, how have you been?"

"Good," he said, "I'm in town and wondering if you want some company."

Cautiously, she was intrigued, "I guess so, can you take a cab? I'll give you the address."

He bought a case of beer and a bottle of vodka and headed over. They hit it off immediately and were both pleasantly surprised with each other's new adult appearance. *The Hound knew he was getting some tonight.*

Not long after, he had her in the bed. "Seduced another one," he thought.

They made love and passed out.

The morning sun shone a beam of light on the Hound's face. As he raised his hand to protect his eyes, he wondered where he was. As he squinted open an eye, he could see an empty bed next to him, the sheets thrown back. He knew someone had been there. It took him a minute to remember who it was, and in his realization, his conscience rushed with both shame and pride at the same time.

The Hound was exhausted. There was a freight train running through his head, and he reeked of alcohol. His eyes were bloodshot and something had died in his mouth. She brought him a coffee and he swore she was Florence Nightingale. Bringing him that coffee was like a nurse bringing him medicine to survive.

He cleaned up and gave her a kiss. Not a deep or meaningful kiss, just a quick thank-you kiss as he knew he would never see her again.

The Hound arrived at the office, just in time for his interviews, and due to his youth he could conceal his condition without suspicion. He put on the charm and wowed them over with his clever wit and his devilish smile. The Hound looked them all in the eye and shook their hands firmly, and always answered their questions with something witty.

By the end of the day the job was his. It seemed like the Hound was finally winning at the game of life.

66

Wanted Dead Or Alive

After getting the job, the company surprised him again with another airline ticket. Even further north. The Hound thought he was going halfway to the North Pole, to a remote town in Northern Canada.

He got off the plane and hailed a cab. "Holiday Inn Downtown." He'd been told to stay there by his new boss, who said it was the nicest hotel in town.

On the drive in he noticed a smell, it smelled like somebody had lit a match and was burning eggshells. The smell raced up his nostrils, like an invading horde, and he gagged at the taste of sulfur. "What's that smell?" He asked the cabbie.

The cabbie, a rough looking 60 or 70 year old, with squinty eyes and a cigarette hanging out of his mouth, said, "That's the smell of money, boy."

The pulp mill was the number one employer in this town, and without it, the town would die. They were willing to overlook whatever stench came from it as long as it kept the town alive. At this point, the town would go bankrupt without the mill running—it was that remote. When something provides all the money for a town, nobody cares what it smells like.

As they approached the hotel the Hound got out of the cab and paid the cabbie. With his suitcase in hand, and his suit flung over his shoulder, he turned around to see two young women punching the shit out of each other. This was no girl's fight—they were throwing hay-makers.

Smack!

The blood flew.

The Hound took a step back and wondered, "Where the hell am I?"

67

Time

He had a company car supplied, a K-car. This was Lee Iacocca's answer to the Japanese auto industry's wild success in North America. He appeared on TV for Chrysler, staking his name on the quality of these cars. It didn't take long to realize it was not worth the hype. Nobody ever heard from him again. This car was a piece of shit.

But for the Hound it was freedom, he had mobility again. He felt like someone had released the Hound.

He made the rounds to all the restaurants who were the clients of *Country Packers*. He introduced himself and took their weekly meat order. At the end of the day he called the order back to head office for it to be delivered to the restaurants later that week.

The Hound liked this job. His territory was massive: on Wednesday he had to drive three hours south, stopping in all the restaurants along the way. When he arrived at the last town on the trip, he spent the night.

He made all his calls and then ended up back at the best hotel and restaurant-bar in town. He got to stay overnight there, so that night the party was on.

It started off at a bar where he hoped to meet some girls; if there were none there he'd head across town to the Overlook Hotel, which had a much bigger bar, rowdier. Cowgirls and divorcees, *Yee-haw!* If you were lucky, you got a cowgirl and were in for quite a ride. Or, you got an older girl that made up for it with willingness.

That place never failed.

After an evening of fun, the Hound would work up an appetite and order egg rolls from his favorite restaurant. When that warm, brown paper bag got dropped off in his hotel room, it was like Christmas morning. Still half drunk, and famished, each bite of those eggrolls was a little piece of Heaven on Earth.

The next day on the way home he'd put on music, and the depression would set in. He'd watch the dark trees fly by outside the window and wonder if the clouds would get heavy enough to snow. The Hound knew he had three hours, and the loneliness was palpable. No matter how much fun he'd had the night before, it seemed to only intensify the sadness the next day. He always saved a joint to help him wallow in the misery. Pushing in his cassette, he drifted into outer space, to the dark side of the moon.

68

Slip Slidin' Away

It was a winter day and the snow was only slightly falling, but the temperature had dropped, enough for the moisture on the roads to form into black ice. This was ice that you couldn't see. It looked as if the road was wet...but it was actually frozen.

The Hound's sales calls were done for the day, so he picked up a case of beer to keep him company on the way home. Driving too fast, in a rush to go nowhere, he lost control of the car and it began to spin. First, slowly, then a full-on twister.

Soon he was hurdling backwards down the highway. A full spin, then another. He could see the sky through the windshield as he hurdled backwards off the road and down into the ravine. "This might end badly," he thought sarcastically.

Smash!

The car came to an abrupt stop, at the base of a 60 foot tree. He opened the door and rolled out onto the wet, cold dirt. He could smell the pine trees, as the cold air bit at his cheeks. He felt his body for broken bones. Luckily, he was in one piece.

The K-car's trunk was gone and the tree was in the back seat. That piece of shit folded like an accordion. To him, that K-car was right where it belonged.

The Hound crawled back out of the ditch, brushing himself off, as he flagged down a car. A middle aged lady pulled over to offer help. The Hound jumped in, oblivious to the wreckage in the ditch. He smiled at her and said, "hey, good lookin'! Let's go get a beer."

That was the Hound, an opportunist. Every interaction in life was an opportunity to gain a thrill and the last disaster was ancient history. Was he a true optimist? Or was denial his greatest blessing?

Later, he'd explain to his boss that he had to swerve to miss a moose.

69

So Lonely

He didn't know many people in town, so he joined a winter baseball league. They used to play in the snow, it was usually minus 20. They had fires going in barrels and hot wine, and after the games when everybody went home the Hound sat by himself around the embers of the dying fires and drank the leftover wine.

He was happy. Happy in his sadness. Alone in the cold with only his melancholy, but happy he had an endless supply of hot wine. Sitting in the field, he knew it was too cold to stay there very long, but he wanted to stay there forever. There were no people left to deal with, and he could just embrace his self-centered pain. Any alcoholic will tell you that self pity, self loathing is like a warm blanket. As long as it's about self, the alcoholic is happy. He could wallow like a pig in the mud, in his sacred pain.

The Hound spent evening after evening in the bars. He would usually start off the evening in the pretty people's bar, where the music was loud and everybody was dressed up, and the dance floor was full. The Hound's words were his bullets, and in this loud environment he was unarmed. He considered himself an intellect and thought these people were beneath him. He convinced himself that they were all shallow and that this kind of social interaction was for the phony people.

Giving up, he would head across the street, to a simple pub: where people could hear each other, and he could ply his trade of wit and humor. Often there'd be nobody there, so he'd swallow his pride, which he didn't have much of, and go two blocks further, to the McDonald Hotel, where all the alcoholics drank. These were his people. He felt at home there and played the bigshot, buying beers for everyone.

He always went home with someone from there, an alcoholic or a drug addict. One night he talked two girls into going home with him. He was never by himself, but he was always alone.

70

Some Girls

One night, after failing to find anybody in the bar, the Hound drove into the darkness towards the edge of town to find the alcoholic crazy woman he knew would sleep with anyone. She was always willing, but he knew she was insane.

Her brand of sex was violent, and she'd scratch his back so hard he'd bleed for a week. It made him feel alive. And powerful. He convinced himself only he made her feel this way and knew he shouldn't be there, but it gave him what he needed. Unfortunately, it gave him a lot more than he bargained for.

He never knew her name and once the Herpes broke out, he never went back. He knew it was her that gave it to him. At first he was angry with her, but then conceded that he deserved it.

He finally went to the doctor. The doctor told him it was going to be like this for the rest of his life.

The Hound would have been devastated if he thought he was going to live much longer. At the self-destructive pace he was on, he'd be lucky to see thirty.

71

Crawling King Snake

The Hound and a couple of his friends from work decided to go on a road trip. They loaded up on beer and took the three-hour ride to the tip of the Alaskan panhandle, to a town called Hyder.

They sang songs and drank beer the whole way, only stopping to pee on the side of the road. This was when the Hound was at his happiest: he had his friends in the front seat driving, while he sat at the back with a case of beer next to him, as he looked out the window at the trees flying by him.

In this moment he felt complete.

If he could just make the world stop here and leave him alone.

As they approached the border, the boys dumped all their empties out into a ditch. Expecting to see customs officials and maybe even police, they sat up, tried to look sober, and were on their best behavior.

Their car came around the corner, as they rolled up towards a sign that said, "Welcome to Alaska."

They all laughed with relief that this town was so remote, there was *nobody* at the border. The pavement ended and they entered the frontier town. There was a hotel with a bar, corner store and a gas station—and nothing else.

The only thing that made this town exist was its geographical location as the southernmost part of America's largest state. The only other thing that made the town famous was called "the screech". It was a 140-proof pure grain alcohol served in the bar. People came from miles around to drink a shot of screech. It was so potent that the custom was to set the empty glass on fire after the patron had been brave enough to drink it. This intrigued the Hound. He asked the bartender, "What was the most anyone had ever drank?"

"Some idiot had three of them," the bartender said. "We had to carry him out of here."

The Hound ordered another.

And another.

The bartender cut him off, sensing that he'd had more than enough. The Hound, unsteady on his feet, staggered over to play pool with his friends. Despite the bartender's refusal, his thirst was still in charge, so he charmed a waitress with a twenty dollar bill to go sneak him another shot so he could break the record.

She obliged and with a devilish smirk and a glint in his

eye, the Hound tossed back his fourth shot.

The room was spinning.

He smoked a cigarette and tried to get his equilibrium back and negotiated with the bartender, "I'll make you a deal: if I can sink this next shot on the pool table, you have to sell me another shot."

The bartender laughed at the man dancing from foot to foot uncontrollably. He could see his eyes were blind as an old dog. "Sure," he said, not expecting him to make it, "take your best shot."

The Hound took up the challenge as he staggered over to the pool table and leaned against it, using all of his will to line up the white ball. It took a couple practice movements sliding the que back and forth between his finger and his thumb. He was sure there were three white balls, so he hit the middle one. To everybody's surprise, he sank the eight-ball in the corner.

Laughing gleefully, the Hound yelled at the bartender, "Set up my fifth shot of screech, you bastard!"

Reluctantly, the bartender poured him his fifth shot of screech. The Hound felt his hand along the bar, trying to grab the glass without falling. He hung on to the side of the bar with his left hand and tilted the white lightning up to his lips, and poured it into the canyon of his soul.

Boom.

He hit the floor like a ton of bricks and tried to get back to his feet, but fell again. He lay on his belly, staring at a dusty wooden plank on the barroom floor.

The Hound had to get outside. He didn't want anyone to see him this way and thought the cool air might help him regain his balance. As the shame was about to overtake him, he began to laugh. He moved his body like a snake, inch by inch he slithered toward the front door, as he belted out, "I'm a Crawling king snake baby, that's exactly what I am," the John Lee Hooker song, attempting to save his dignity. As long as he was laughing at the absurdity of his condition, he felt no shame.

Out the front door he crawled, slithering down the steps onto the dirt street. He went another ten or twenty yards, leaving a trail in the dirt behind him like an anaconda. His friends followed him out and helped him to his feet. They braced him up and headed to the hotel, leaning him against a post as they got their room.

As they were making their way toward their rented room, the Hound broke loose from them and sprinted straight into somebody else's hotel room door. He hit it with such force, the door flew open, and he landed at the foot of the bed, startling the young couple that were asleep.

The man sat up in bed and yelled at him, "What the hell man?"

The Hound grabbed one of the man's shoes off the floor, and began biting at it and growling at the man like a drunken, mad dog.

As his friends dragged him out of the room, a bunch of locals attacked the boys. Fists flew and the boys were overpowered.

They dragged them back into their car and ran them out of town. One of the boys somehow drove them back across the border and they pulled over to the side of the road and fell asleep in the car.

When the morning sun attacked them, the car was full of stink and alcohol. The Hound pried open one eye, and felt like he'd been hit by a train.

As the boys woke up and got ready to leave, the Hound said from the back seat, "Damn that was fun!"

72

Do Ya Think I'm Sexy?

The Hound continued this cycle of drunkenness, drug use and casual sex. He was constantly in the pursuit of sexual partners.

Everyone qualified.

After all, he knew he could have sex and create pleasure with any shape or form, and it was the emotional validation that he was seeking, not the status or beauty. Not intimacy or love, but adoration, praise and gratitude. These are the things that filled the hole within him.

But that hole was insatiable; he could only feel full for a few moments. Then the hole would reappear, and the instinct to hunt for the things that might fill it again would overpower him.

This is why he burned through partners like he did cases of beer. Once he had satisfied that person, it was like all the juice he could get had been squeezed from them. And he needed a new piece of fruit.

He was willing to get the rush from anyone that would get naked with him and let him seduce them, undress them, pleasure them, let them adore his body, praise his penis, exhaust them in pleasure, until all they could say was "Thank you." This not only satisfied his adult ego, but helped heal the 12-year-old boy from the shower shaming.

It could be the checkout girl at the grocery store, the waitress at the bar, the middle-aged housewife in the liquor store line-up. His good looks and charm were honed to perfection.

He was a weapon. A weapon of mass seduction.

73

I Won't Back Down

The day-to-day monotony of a job was losing its appeal. He had to stay sober for hours, and it just felt like an interruption of what he really wanted to do with his time. He wanted to be drunk and high and hunt for sexual gratification.

One day he met a guy named Travis, who told him about his business in the pest control industry. He worked for a big company, and he wanted to start his own business.

Once the Hound realized that the clients he needed were all the same clients the Hound had: restaurants, hospitals—anywhere that had a kitchen, really—the Hound said "Let's go into business together. I'll sell all the accounts, and you'll service them."

They shook hands, and set out to conquer the North.

The Hound had no trouble switching all his *Country*

Packers clients, who spent thousands with him on meat, over to a minor contract for pest control. So, in the span of a couple of weeks, he had converted them all to his and Travis's company.

One day, the phone rang. It was his boss from the *Country Packers*. "What the hell are you doing out there? Did you start a pest control company? That's a conflict of interest. You can't do both businesses at the same time!"

The Hound didn't think it should be a problem but when his boss showed up, he was fired. Staying true to his impulsive nature, he took all his *Country Packers* sales information, including all the clients personal information, and all the history, and all the invoices and bills and accounts, and with his boss watching, he threw them into the mighty river and said to his ex-boss:

"Now you *have a conflict of interest!*"

74

Spiders And Snakes

The Hound became a full time pest control man. Now he was free to be stoned every day, and wear jeans and a T-shirt. He could fly under the radar, he could be incognito. He was no longer the polished salesman any more. He looked like a regular working Joe.

Now he could be a wolf in sheep's clothing.

He bought an old Toyota pickup truck, with a lift kit and big tires. The passenger's door had to be held closed with a coat hanger, and the red truck had more rust than paint. It was a perfect vehicle for *Pest Control*.

The Hound would now become a hunter. He killed ants and wasps and fleas and rats. He learned all about the pesticides and the poisons. He loved to scare the clients with horror stories of infestations and rabies, then charge them twice what he should have. He'd kick them out of their house and eat their food and watch their TV. Most of the killing could be done fast. A spray here, a poison there, a couple traps at worst. *This,* the Hound thought, *was the best job in the world.*

75

The Sound Of Silence

The Hound had his own apartment, and a lady down the hall had given him a kitten. She saw that the Hound needed company.

He had never had a cat before and his dad had never let him have any pets in the house. The Hound went to the store and bought cat food and kitty litter, and a little shovel to scoop the cat's poop out of the cat litter. The lady told him this is what he would need.

Everyday the Hound would get home and look forward to the kitten bouncing over to him. *You look like a Sydney to me, I think I'll call you Syd.*

This little kitten made the Hound so happy. This cat was his best friend.

Syd was a Burmese Longhair. He would sleep on his neck at night, which the Hound loved...until Syd was a full grown cat.

The Hound had to push him off his neck at night, or he'd suffocate him, but he didn't push him too far away. He liked the feel of the soft hair and the sound of his purring.

When he moved in with Travis, to save on rent money, he insisted on bringing Syd with him. It was a deal breaker.

Travis had his own cat. A Siamese cat, and the cats hated one another.

One day the Hound came home, and Syd was nowhere to be found. Travis seemed strangely empathetic. It wasn't like him to show any compassion, but he actually went out that night and helped the Hound search for Syd.

They went up and down the back alleys, calling for Syd. "Syd! Here Syd! Sydney!"

The cat was nowhere to be found and the Hound was suspicious. Syd never left home before. He couldn't prove it, but he suspected Travis had something to do with it.

Travis hated Syd.

76

Switchin' To Glide

Later that year, Travis told the Hound that his brother, Al, was getting out of prison, and he was going to come and stay with him for a while. Travis and the Hound shared a three story old house in the industrial part of town. It was beat up, but it had a lot of rooms. The Hound had moved into the attic. There was still a spare room downstairs for the new guest, but that wasn't the first question on the Hound's mind.

"Prison?" the Hound asked. "What was he in prison for?"

"Bank robbery."

"Shit," the Hound was surprised, but was up for anything.

When Al showed up, he didn't look like anything the Hound would have imagined. He had short hair and a baby face. Except for the muscles and tattoos, you could have mistaken him for a boy scout.

He was very friendly, and the Hound and Al became drinking buddies that went out to the bars every night. Travis had a girlfriend, so he stayed home. Besides, Travis was an ex-military guy and was way too uptight for Al and the Hound.

Out in the bars, the Hound would charm the ladies, and help Al pick up a woman by telling her: "My friend Al here hasn't had sex in ten years, would you be so kind as to help him out of his current dilemma?"

The Hound liked to end the night by drinking flaming sambucas. This was a shot of ouzo that was set on fire, and as long as you tipped the glass fast enough, the fire would not burn your face. If, however, you hesitated, you could lose an eyebrow.

The Hound *loved* this kind of danger. Self-inflicted.

Many nights the Hound and Al brought women home to the house and carried the party on.

Travis hated this, and was growing ever more jealous of the Hound's lifestyle and his relationship with his brother. The Hound was a wild and beautiful creature, he seemed fearless and charmed everybody he came in contact with.

But one night, his charm failed him, and Travis's jealousy would escalate towards murder.

77

Twilight Zone

Travis's girlfriend confessed to the Hound that Travis had shot Syd. He was a sadist. He held that beautiful cat by the scruff of the neck and shot it in the head and threw it in a dumpster, and then helped the Hound look for him.

Considering their friendship over, the Hound began to strategize on how to leave town. He'd had enough of Travis and they began to argue about business and money.

There was tension in the house.

One night, after the Hound and Al came home from the bar, Travis appeared in the front room with his army rifle, he loaded the chamber and cocked the gun.

Raising it to his shoulder, he pointed the rifle at the Hound, who was sitting on the couch. "You have been sleeping with my girlfriend, haven't you?" Travis said.

The Hound could see the craziness in his eyes and

Thirst | 195

realized he was in trouble. This danger was real. "Absolutely not!" and for once, he was not lying.

Travis didn't believe him, and told him that this would be the Hound's last day on earth. He told the Hound to write out his last will and testament.

The Hound wouldn't do it. He just kept saying, "Put the gun down, Travis. You don't want to do this. I might be dead—but you will have to spend the rest of your life in prison."

"Enough! Don't try to sell me!" barked Travis, his eyes now starting to roll into his head as he clearly started to go insane. "Shut the fuck up!" He took aim and looked down the barrel at the Hound.

Time slowed down. It was like everything was happening in slow motion. He looked up at the barrel of the gun and then…

Bang!

The shot rang out - barely missing the Hound by a fraction, it flew through the window, across the street, into the hardware store, and set off the alarms.

The Hound reeled in disbelief, as his right ear rang from the force of the bullet's near-miss. He couldn't believe he was still alive.

Just then, Al tackled his crazed brother from behind, and the Hound pounced on top of them. Travis was stronger than they expected. It took the Hound and Al all of their might to hold him down.

Al took the gun away from Travis as the Hound ran down the street. He stood a block away, a safe distance, and watched all the police cars descend on the house.

Travis was taken away in handcuffs.

The Hound went back inside and thanked Al for helping to save him. "I hate this house. Let's go get a beer and pick up some women."

78

Lola

The next morning, with Travis still in jail, the police wanted the Hound to make a statement. The Hound wanted nothing more to do with Travis. Al suggested that they leave town. This sounded like the right thing to do.

So they packed the old Toyota truck and made their getaway.

They had a little money, but no plan. They were hell-bent on getting to Vancouver. It was a 9 hour drive and with two cases of beer, they were going to arrive in the city in good form.

Al knew the city, it was where he lived before prison. So he gave the Hound directions. Al knew where he wanted to go. "Take a left here," Al said, "Now a right," as they wound their way into the heart of the city. "Two more blocks. Go left there."

As they turned the corner, the Hound could see the prostitutes on the sidewalk. Al said, "Pull up to that one!" and he rolled the window down as the prostitute leaned in.

"Hi boys, you want some company tonight?"

For a change, Al took the lead. He was on fire, crackling like a whip. The Hound had never seen him this excited.

Then the Hound took a closer look. Something seemed different. She was beautiful, yet she had big hands, and a large Adam's apple.

The Hound, concerned his friend might not realize the situation, leaned over to inform him. "Al, Al," he whispered, "She's a man."

Al turned around with a grin and said, "I know! Tits and a cock! The best of both worlds."

79

La Grange

That night Al would convince the Hound to go and meet all the prostitutes.

The Hound was up for anything, once he was over his surprise, he was quite curious.

They went to get something to eat. It was Al, the Hound, and five or six ladies of the evening. The Hound noticed how pretty they were.

Al convinced the women to go back to their apartment. Three or four of them shared it. It was a big apartment, the Hound surmised they must make a lot of money.

The Hound wanted to get the hell out of there. It was fun, but it was too weird to stay any longer. Al said, "Go ahead, I'm staying here. These ladies need a protector, and I'm their new pimp."

The women all giggled and seemed to like Al's idea.

The Hound laughed and said, "To each his own, buddy! Take care of yourself." So he gave Al a hug and said good night to the ladies.

The Hound rode the elevator down to the lobby. As he pushed open the doors and walked out onto the damp Vancouver night, he could smell the pine trees and the rain. For the first time in his life, he could go anywhere he wanted. He just had no idea where that was.

80

Boys In The Bright White Sports Car

Looking for work, the Hound spotted an ad in the paper for a car salesman. So he made his way downtown. He was only 22, but he was certain he could sell cars even though he didn't know anything about them. He thought that all he needed was charm, and he had that in spades.

The car dealership that had placed the ad was a Honda store. They told him that he was too young. Undeterred, he walked across the street into the Nissan dealership and this time, he didn't take no for an answer.

After his best attempts at being confident, with a firm handshake, eye contact, and a big smile, the Hound explained that it would be a big mistake for them to miss landing a talent like him; that what he didn't have in experience, he'd make up for in hard work, and that his superpower was persuasion.

The sales manager could see there was potential as he had that *je ne sais quoi*, that special-something, so he decided to give him a chance. What neither of those men knew was that the Hound was destined to work at this particular car dealership. For fate was aligning him with the love of his life. Marie was the CFO, at work in her office just down the hall. They never met that day, as the Hound was given a car from the manager. "This is your demo, if you learn how to sell these, I'll let you drive anything you want."

The Hound looked over and saw a white 300 ZX sports car.

By the end of the first month he would be driving it.

81

Love Struck Baby

The Hound was a natural. He sold more cars in the first month than anybody else in the dealership. Even the namesake of the dealership, the grandson-who had three generations of clients-couldn't outsell the Hound. The Hound had three weapons working for him: charm, persistence, and deception.

He knew just what to say, had a knack for sensing the customers' needs, and maintained the perfect charisma to close deal after deal. He weaved his magic with his silver tongue; he could hear the girls in the office giggling whenever they would eavesdrop.

One day he saw her sitting at her desk. With her shoulder length blonde hair and green eyes, she looked like a vision. She had a strong, beautiful face, and she looked in charge in her green dress. It was Marie.

Marie was holding court, as the men surrounded her

desk. One was the general manager who ran the store. The other two were bankers, and one was from the Nissan factory. Together they formed the power circle, and she was in the center of it.

It all fell into place. He knew at that moment, she could save him and that he would love her forever. His heart was full of passion and admiration. He felt something he had never felt before.

It was Divine love.

82

Pride And Joy

Every day, the Hound made an excuse to go in and talk to Marie. He would ask her about his check, or taxes, but soon enough he disclosed his true desire. He asked Marie out on a date.

"Absolutely……..*NOT*," Marie replied, "I don't date anyone at work."

After several failed attempts, one day the Hound came into work hungover. He'd lost his confidence and his bravado. The alcohol from the night before had beaten it out of him. He was vulnerable. He went into Marie's office to ask for his check. His eyes were bloodshot, and his head was bowed. He didn't ask her out this time.

Marie could see he was a beaten man. Her compassion took over. "Okay," Marie said, "you can take me out on one date."

At dinner, they spoke for several hours on many subjects. They matched wits and were intellectual equals. The Hound had respect for her that he had never had for women before, and she was intrigued with his mind. As the evening ended, and the Hound walked Marie to her car, he fell into an old, familiar habit of trying to escalate the relationship to sex, immediately.

He leaned in to kiss her goodnight, and pulled her tight to him. He pressed himself assertively into her. She pushed him off, "Take it easy—you're not getting any of that action tonight!" she said. The Hound was taken aback by his rejection. That didn't happen often. This made him want Marie even more.

They worked and partied together as one. They became inseparable. It was 1987. It was their summer of love. They had the t-roofs off the 300 ZX and they raced around the city in the warm summer sun, with the Hound singing to her.

83

Magic Man

Marie was 29, and the Hound was only 22 but he lied to her, fearing she wouldn't date him if she knew how young he was. He told her he was 28.

One night Marie cooked dinner for him, she did it effortlessly. She threw together some vegetables and meat, stirred it all in a pan, and somehow it turned out delicious. The Hound had never really seen someone whip together a dinner like that before.

He was falling in love with her. She still hadn't let him make love to her, but they were close now. They felt like a couple.

The Hound went to have a shower, and when he was finished, he pulled the curtain back, and Marie was standing there with a towel. She hadn't seen him naked before. She pretended not to look, but he was sure she did. He took the towel and started to dry himself off, but he couldn't hide his excitement. They smiled at each other, and she took him by the hand, and led him into the bedroom.

They moved together like they'd done it for centuries. Like they were old lovers, from a time long ago, who had found each other again.

They made love like they had done it a thousand times before.

This scared the hell out of Marie.

84

She's The One

The Hound decided he was never leaving.

Marie had told him she had two kids, but they were away with their father for the summer. The Hound couldn't contemplate at that moment the size of the responsibility and difficulties he would have in trying to become a parent. To him, everything was fun and games, and he told Marie, "Any kids of yours are friends of mine."

One day, her ex-husband slid open the window to their bedroom and pushed the two kids onto the bed. Marie wouldn't answer the door, and her ex-husband knew she was home. So he pushed those two kids in like they dropped from the sky and the Hound's life would never be the same again.

85

Bad To The Bone

The Hound told Marie about Al, his bank robber friend who was pimping for the prostitutes downtown now. Marie thought that was hilarious, and she told him to invite Al and his girlfriend, Jaimie, to come for dinner.

It was a dinner party, and one of the mechanics from work, a German fellow named Dirk, after a few too many schnapps, became quite flirtatious with Jaimie. He had no idea she was a transwoman, but he was attracted to her. Jaimie started to flirt with him, as she saw the humor in his unawareness and gave them all a wink. She saw this uptight German mechanic making a pass at her, too drunk to realize she wasn't exactly who he thought she was.

They all shared a good laugh and called Dirk a taxi.

One day the Hound went to visit Al and have a beer with him. "How are things going, Al?"

"Not so good. I've started robbing people on the street."

"What?!" asked the Hound.

"I walk up to people on the sidewalk, ask them if they know what time it is. And when they stop to tell me, I yell, 'Give me your money!' in the loudest meanest voice I can. And they all give me their money. I don't know why I'm doing it. The girls make me lots of money and I think I'm just bored."

The Hound pleaded with him. "Al, don't do that! You're going to end up back in jail!"

The next time the Hound saw him, Al was knocking on the Hound's door. When the Hound opened it, Al rushed in and dumped a bag of money on the floor, two handguns and a ski mask. "I robbed a bank today, it was awesome! I need you to hide this shit for me."

"Are you crazy? I have kids in here. I can't do that."

"Well just take some of the money, I'll come for it later," Al said.

The Hound couldn't refuse that, so he hid the money in his closet, and Al disappeared into the night, with the guns, the mask, and the gleeful spirit of a child at Christmas.

The next week Al showed up again, this time with a bag of pharmaceuticals. He had robbed a pharmacy and was like a cat bringing home a kill to get praise. The Hound didn't want this dead animal in his house.

So Al took it all and left. The next time the Hound talked to Al he was calling him from prison.

Al told him he robbed the pharmacy two more times, and by the third time, the police were waiting for him. He told the Hound he was relieved. It was too hard on the outside, too many choices. In prison, life was structured. He liked that better.

Sometime around Christmas, the Hound and Marie were watching TV and the news came on

"Break out at Prison!" .

There was a breakout at one of the local prisons. From the footage, the Hound could see the sign. The name was familiar

The Hound looked at Marie and said, "That's where Al is."

Just then, the phone rang.

86

Jailbreak

It was Al. He and seven other inmates had made makeshift knives out of razor blades and toothbrushes. Together, they overpowered the guards and made their escape.

Al had gone straight for Jaimie. And they were on the run. "Bonnie and Clyde," Al said. "We're just like Bonnie and Clyde."

Marie and the Hound watched as all six other inmates were caught that week, mostly at their mother's house.

They laughed. "Crazy!" They couldn't think of anywhere to go except back to their mom's house. Not Al and Jaimie, though. They called once from Edmonton, and another time from Montreal. Al said they had to leave Edmonton, rednecks would freak out when they discovered Jaimie was trans.

But Montreal was a much bigger and wilder town. It was

on the Saint Lawrence Seaway, so the drugs poured in and organized crime ruled the town.

The Hound told Al, "That's good, stay out there!"

Al was already making noises about coming back to Vancouver. "Don't do it," said the Hound, "They'll catch you again."

But Jaimie and Al were homesick, and the Montreal winters were harsher than they were used to - too cold for a street walker. It wasn't long before the Hound got his final phone call from Al. He was back in Vancouver, and was arrested after a car chase for a bank robbery.

Al told the Hound, "Don't come visit me, I'm going to prison forever. Get on with your life."

The Hound did just that, he never heard from either of them ever again.

87

Madman Across The Water

The Hound's drinking didn't stop, he got drunk every night. For the most part, he was a friendly and happy drunk.

The kids didn't accept him. The young boy, Marcus, was dark and suspicious, and made sure the Hound *knew* he wasn't his father. The girl, Jessica, was a year older than Marcus. She was outwardly friendly to the Hound, but much more calculating in her desire to kill him.

The Hound took it upon himself to be the best stepdad he could be. He promised Jessica and Marcus a better life, a bigger house, and a future together. The kids had heard that before.

He was still doing well at work, but the drinking was starting to create depression for him. The job seemed monotonous and the joy of winning had gotten stale, so he needed a change.

He moved the family out to the suburbs and got a job selling furniture at a national chain called *The Furniture Store*. It was a fresh start, and the Hound decided to quit drinking.

After all, he was a father now and he wanted to be a good stepfather for those kids, and a good partner for Marie.

So he put the plug in the jug, got in shape through running and weightlifting, and even cut his hair short. He was putting himself through his own bootcamp and he started to become the best salesman he could.

The Hound managed to stay sober and become the top salesman at *The Furniture Store*. He was a selling machine, setting a one-day sales record for the company. Having sold so much furniture, the Hound felt bad for the guys on the loading dock. When he learned he had set the record, the Hound felt obliged to buy some beer and throw a party.

The dock workers, the other salespeople, and the Hound's bosses were all invited over to the house. They had a small basement with a pool table - the party was on.

It never occurred to the Hound that he would be losing his sobriety. He had made it three months sober. Now, drunk on glory, it was an easy slip back to the bottle.

Basking in his glory as the man of the hour, he couldn't believe it when people wanted to leave. "This party is not ending!" He said, locking the door.

88

One Of My Turns

The Hound was drunk and he did not want his reign to end. He was the king of the world.

Soon, the men started to try to physically remove him from the door. The wives were outraged, and his bosses tried to talk some sense into him. In a blind black out, he started to punch his guests. He managed to grab hold of a pool ball and threw it at one guy's head. It just missed him, and embedded into the drywall. *Thump.*

Marie appeared and tried to calm the Hound down. But in his condition he didn't recognize her. He pushed her backwards, and she fell, hitting her head on the concrete floor.

The others gang-tackled him, holding him down until the police arrived.

Once he was in handcuffs he regained his awareness.

Guilt and shame blanketed him.

What the fuck did I do?

He was back in jail. Again.

89

Lithium

In front of the judge the next morning, he had no explanation for his behavior. The judge tried to get to the motive, but there was none apparent.

It was crazy.

The judge sent him to a psychiatrist. "Let's get a diagnosis, before I sentence you."

The Hound went back home to beg for Marie's forgiveness, explaining to her that the judge thought he might have a mental illness. So an appointment was set up to see a psychiatrist. The Hound hoped this would ease Marie's opinion of him. Anything to explain away his violent actions.

Off to see the psychiatrist, hoping for a key to understanding his behavior.

In the psychiatrist's office, he asked, "Tell me about what happened. Do you often get these crazy moods? How much do you regularly drink?"

The Hound lied. "I drink a few beers once in a while."

The psychiatrist surmised, "Sounds like you are manic-depressive. Bipolar disorder."

The Hound was thrilled. He had a *reason* for his insanity.

It wasn't his fault.

There was a chemical imbalance! Not a lapse in moral character.

This made him so happy.

The doctor prescribed lithium. The Hound asked him if he could still have a few drinks while on the medication.

The doctor explained that the medicine worked better if he didn't.

What the Hound heard, was that it was okay to drink.

90

Born To Run

It was time to move again.

It must be this town and all the losers in it. The truth was nobody would hire him in that town after word got around.

The Hound needed a fresh start, so he convinced Marie to move to the town she grew up in. "So you can be close to your family," he told her. This was his attempt at hiding his selfish motive under a benevolent gesture. Selling her on having to move the whole family to another town because of his drunken lunacy.

So off they went on the road to victory.

The Hound got a job selling Nissans again. Not trusting himself, they rented a house two towns away. If the Hound fell into any more drinking trouble, he wanted some space between the crime scene and his home.

Getting up early, the Hound made the hour drive to work down the two-lane highway, next to the lake. On the way home, a case of beer kept him company. By the time he rolled into his driveway, he would go straight to bed and pass out drunk.

He drank every night. In the morning, even after a shower, the alcohol would seep out of his pores. He became depressed. The melancholy was with him every morning. On the drive to work, as the road approached a sharp turn above the lake, he imagined holding his steering wheel straight and sailing off of the cliff in some grandiose death scene. This somehow seemed a logical way to end the suffering.

The pain he felt deep inside him, the pain that came from nowhere. There was so much for him to look forward to. He had a beautiful woman who loved him. He had kids who were trying to put up with his haphazard behavior. He found his niche with sales job after sales job.

Yet all of it was at the mercy of a demon that kept finding new ways to reappear. Every alcoholic and addict feels chained to this anchor; pulling them into the depths of despair. With no escape in sight, they yearn for the drowning. Anything to find peace. Even death.

91

Running On Empty

He was selling a lot of cars, more than this little dealership had ever seen. He wasn't limited by inconvenient things like the truth. If he saw somebody liked the car, he would pull the price tag out of it before the customer saw it. Then he'd make sure that all their dreams would come true, as he made them imagine long road trips with their loved ones. Once he had them convinced this was the car for them, he'd tell them it was much more expensive than it actually was.

One time he got 5,000 dollars above the asking price and in those days, that was unheard of. His boss marveled at both his ability and his larceny. They loved the money, but they'd have to keep a close eye on the Hound.

One day he convinced his boss to let him take an expensive vehicle on a holiday, and he and Marie headed back towards the coast. They picked up an old friend, and they all got drunk. They ended up skinny dipping in the ocean.

The Hound never put his clothes back on, and got in behind the wheel.

Marie and her friend got dressed.

The Hound decided they were going to drive to California that night. It was a three-day drive. The Hound didn't think that through. Marie loved the adventure. She was up for anything.

As they approached the US border, the Hound rolled his window down and pulled up to the customs officer.

"Where are you guys going?"

"Headed to Disneyland," said the Hound.

"Have you got anything to declare?"

The Hound, as naked as the day he was born, smiled and said, "Not a thing."

The customs officer couldn't see below his bare chest and couldn't imagine that he would be naked.

Assuming everything was normal, they were waved through the border and all laughed hysterically.

A few hours later they approached Seattle. Marie and her friend were already asleep. The Hound was speeding and nodding off when the freeway split in two directions. They missed the bridge pillar by a foot. Another brush with the Grim Reaper, that would have killed all of them.

That woke him up, and he managed to drive halfway to Oregon where he finally pulled over into a rest stop to pass out. He climbed into the back of the pathfinder and curled up with Marie.

In the morning they all awoke confused. They had no idea where they were but they certainly weren't in Disneyland.

So they turned the car around and headed back north. The Hound was still half drunk, so he pulled over, told Marie he was going to go catch a cow, and ran through the field naked, chasing one.

Luckily for the cow, the Hound was too slow.

92

Radar Love

A few miles up the road a policeman pulled them over. The Hound was dressed by then and when the police discovered it was not his vehicle, but belonged to a car dealership in Canada, the cops called the dealership.

When the Hound's boss heard the situation, he couldn't believe the Hound had taken his car that far away but he wanted him back to sell more cars, so he told the policeman it was fine.

Back home they went, and the Hound returned to work.

Soon he was bored, and he told his boss that *he* should be running the company. The Hound was only 25 but was by far the most talented person in the company.

So the boss told him he owned two stores, a Nissan dealership and a Toyota dealership. He told the Hound he could run the morning sales meeting for all the salespeople and if he did a good job running the sales meeting, he'd make him the manager of one of the stores.

The Hound headed home, excited to tell Marie about his new opportunity. That night Marie's brother showed up with a huge bag of cocaine. Instead of getting a good night's sleep for his great opportunity in the morning, the Hound sat up, freebasing cocaine all night.

Freebasing was what they called 'crack' before crack was invented; they would get a spoon full of ammonia, and heat it on the stove, and then pour the cocaine into the bubbling liquid, and it would cook the cocaine into a rock. Then you could smoke that rock in a pipe and it felt like every cell in your body was submerged in nirvana.

The inner peace and quiet was life altering. It was a body stone. After exhaling, his entire body went limp, his head tilted back, and he stared at the ceiling as a smile appeared on his face. He couldn't move, he was going to be in this position for a few minutes now, no matter what was happening around him.

They cooked and smoked all night, chasing that elusive feeling from the first high. Rock after rock vanished into the pipe as the feeling lingered on. They chased the dragon and got stoned out of their minds, until the entire bag was gone.

Then the Hound remembered he had a career changing event in a couple hours.

93

Beth

Soon the sun was coming through the window, and the Hound realized he had to get cleaned up and get to work.

He was exhausted.

He showered and dressed and sped into the dealership. He stood in front of everyone, and surprised himself by dazzling them with charm and humor and giving them tips on strategic selling.

They all applauded and cheered.

And when he looked over at the owner he knew he had the job.

He told his boss he would start tomorrow, and went straight home to bed.

The next day he was the sales director of the Toyota store, he was only 25.

He built his team and they sold more Toyotas that year than ever before.

Finally he knew the world saw his greatness. His arrogance grew and his ego knew no bounds.

Each night after work he'd go across the street to the pub, call Marie and tell her he'd be home in an hour. He drank beer, played pool, and chased women.

Then he'd call her, and tell her again he'd be home in an hour.

Hours later, he'd call her again and say he'd be home in an hour.

By midnight, he'd call her and invite her down.

She never came.

By the time he'd got home, she was asleep and this became the pattern.

94

Hot Rod Lincoln

It was Marie's son Marcus's 9th birthday, and the Hound was supposed to be home for supper at five. There was going to be cake and presents that Marie had prepared for little Marcus's party.

The Hound decided to go and have one beer first before he drove home.

Four hours later, drunk, he had missed the party.

Driving home, he was pulled over and charged with his second drunk driving offense.

This was the least of his troubles.

Marie was mad.

95

Gimme Some Lovin

Marie told the Hound it would be better if he was single. She'd had enough.

When the Hound saw that she might be serious, he took his sunglasses off, looked her deep in her eyes, and said, "Let's make a baby."

96

Let's Get It On

The Hound knew this was Marie's soft spot. The other two kids were almost teenagers now, and this would be their first baby together.

Although they weren't married, agreeing to a baby would show his commitment and love to her. After all, the Hound couldn't live without her. He needed her, so he'd have to move fast to show her how serious he was.

Marie had an IUD as a contraceptive. The Hound thought it would be romantic to take her to the hospital immediately to have it removed. The first hospital they went to refused, so he bought a case of beer and drove an hour and a half to the next town. At this hospital, he was able to convince them.

That night, they drove out on the backroads into the forest; climbed into the back of their four runner. Under a starlit sky, their son was conceived.

97

Wild Horses

Things were looking up. He was a sales manager at the Toyota dealership. They had a new house, Marie was pregnant and the Hound had found an ice hockey team.

On Marie's daughter Jessica's birthday, the Hound decided to do something grandiose: the young teenager loved horses. So the Hound bought her one and decided to ride it home.

He had never ridden a horse before, but up the street he came. He imagined he was a knight on a white stallion but in reality, it was a small horse, and it was feisty. The horse sensed that the Hound did not know what he was doing.

The Hound had arranged to have Marie bring Jessica outside to see the arriving hero riding up with the horse: a grand gesture.

He imagined a graceful entrance and hand-off.

As the horse got closer to the house, it broke into a gallop. The Hound was holding on for dear life, terrified. As he bounced by the house at full speed, he could hear Jessica's delighted screams. She was thrilled with the horse but Marie could see the Hound was in trouble.

The horse slammed on his brakes, and threw the Hound head over heels into the ditch.

He was okay. Embarrassed, but relieved as Jessica took the horse away.

That was the last time the Hound would ever ride a horse.

98

A Hard Rain's A-Gonna Fall

It was Christmas Eve and Marie was eight-months pregnant. The Hound thought she should have a ring. He wasn't going to get married, but she should look like she was a proper woman while delivering the baby.

So after drinking heavily the Hound caught a ride to the mall with his friend, just before it closed. He needed other people to drive him, as he had lost his license for drunk driving. He went to the jewelry counter and thought he had about 1,500 dollars left on his credit card. So he looked at rings priced less than that.

He had it narrowed down to two, and when he gave one of them back, the store clerk turned away from him and forgot he still had another one.

It was busy, and there were lots of people in the store, so it must have slipped her mind. The Hound closed his fist on the last ring and knew just what he wanted to do.

He could walk out with the ring and still have 1,500 dollars on his credit card to drink.

The next morning Marie was thrilled. The ring fit perfectly. She loved it.

99

Sweet Child O' Mine

The month passed by, and the baby was about to be born. The Hound watched the news as the Gulf War broke out, eating pizza and drinking beer until it was time for him to go into the delivery room.

He stood by Marie, in awe of her bravery and strength as she pushed his son into the world. He was perfect. The Hound was humbled for the first time in his life. He saw Marie do something he would never have the courage to do. He was reminded of who had the strength in their relationship. Marie was in charge. She deserved to be.

Max was born, quietly crying. The nurses washed the blood from his skin, wrapped him in a blanket and handed him to the Hound. His eyes filled with tears, his heart was full of love like it had never been before. He saw this little guy as a part of him, some deeper reason to stay alive. He was a bundle of hope.

The Hound went home and drank all night and phoned everybody he could think of. He was so proud of his son. He swore to himself that night that he would do everything he could to look after him.

100

Breaking The Law

A week later, back at work, the Hound got a phone call from Marie. "I think you're in trouble, honey. A policeman just came to the house and took my ring. He's on his way to get you right now."

The Hound was full of shame and fear. For he knew he was guilty. Guilty of stealing the ring, guilty of embarrassing his boss, and most of all: guilty of breaking Marie's heart. Again.

The policeman introduced himself. "I knew you did it the next day, as the girl from the store recognized your picture in the Toyota advertisement on the back page of the paper."

"That's him! The sales manager!" she'd told him.

But the policeman had compassion, and didn't want to upset Marie until after she had the baby.

This touched the Hound. It seemed like an honorable thing for the policeman to do and it was now his turn to do the honorable thing.

He knew just what he had to do.

Admitting his wrongdoing to the policeman, he would surrender voluntarily, not needing to be handcuffed.

The detective agreed and said he'd wait for him at the police station in an hour.

The hound went in to see his boss, explaining that he was being charged for theft, so he was going to resign.

His boss asked him, "Did you do it?"

"Yes," said the Hound, "I was drunk and I did it."

His boss said, "You have so much talent, but you have a drinking problem. You need to quit."

The Hound respected his boss, but hated him for that comment. *Fuck you,* he thought. *You don't get to tell me whether I drink or not.*

The Hound headed to the police station, to get booked and fingerprinted. As he walked in, he tried to act cool; head held high, smiling at everybody.

The officer spread his hand out, rolling his thumb on the ink and then rolled that fingerprint onto another paper. He did that with each one of the Hound's fingers. The Hound was now booked for theft and was registered in the system.

He made his way home to apologize to Marie.

He felt so much shame and regret.
But not enough to quit drinking.

101

Back On The Chain Gang

The next day the Hound called Eddie, an old friend of his, to go drinking. Eddie picked him up in his cheap truck, and off to the bar they went.

Eddie explained to him they could make money seal-coating driveways. "I know how to do it, it's easy. I'll show you."

They went to the hardware store, bought two brooms, a pail of seal-coat, and he already had a drill to mix them. They drove around the wealthier neighborhoods looking for driveways that were old and cracked up. When they found one, the Hound went into action.

He knocked on the door. "Hello ma'am! We happened to be in the neighborhood doing a big job, and we have one pail left over, and we noticed your driveway could use it. Would you like us to do it right now?"

"Well how much would it cost me?" the lady said.

"Well, regularly it can be close to a thousand dollars. But since we have leftovers, we'll do it for just the labor. Give us 200 dollars cash, and we'll do it."

Of course she agreed and the guys went to work, spreading that oil all over the driveway with their brooms. It only took them about half an hour, and the job was done.

The Hound got the 200 dollars, and went straight to the pub.

This was the daily routine: wake up hungover, buy a pail of seal-coat, and start knocking on doors. The Hound's charm and enthusiasm always got them a job before noon, and they were in the pub every afternoon.

Marie started to get concerned as the bills were piling up but the Hound didn't seem to care.

One night the Hound threw a party at the house. Some of his old friends from the car dealership were there. After twenty beers, the Hound was in true form.

As the evening was winding down, the Hound had talked one of the women outside into his truck, parked in front of the house by the front door.

He convinced the woman to have sex, even though there was a house full of people. Balls deep, the Hound was busted, as Marie opened the door to say goodnight to some of their guests.

Marie kept her cool, but everyone knew what just happened.

The Hound went back inside, up to bed and was gone the next morning before she could wake up.

It was never mentioned again. Marie could tell what was going on. His drinking had become acute and his behavior had become completely unpredictable.

He was in the final stages of alcoholism. He was completely submerged in his disease.

102

Ain't That a Shame

One day the Hound came home to find two plain-clothes policemen, sitting in his front room.

"I'm Sergeant Bouchard and this is constable Campbell. We're here to investigate a sexual assault allegation."

The Hound racked his mind for what he might have done. Apparently he had exposed himself on the beach. Drunk one day, he saw a couple of girls he liked, got an erection and showed it to them. He probably thought it was funny at the time, but they called the police.

One of the girls knew who he was, and filed the complaint.

The police could see that the Hound was drunk. He asked them if it was okay if he drank the last of his beer.

They told him he could finish one more, but they were taking him downtown.

He asked if he'd get home that night but they said that it would be up to the judge.

They put him in the back of the squad car, as Marie and the kids watched him be hauled off to jail.

103

Smells Like Teen Spirit

Still in jail, the Hound realized he wasn't appearing before any judge that night. They had lied. The Hound would have been pissed off at them, but he knew he deserved to be there. He curled up on the steel slab, used his arm as a pillow, and tried to convince himself everything was alright.

In the morning they charged him. He was getting fingerprinted again, and he looked up to see one of the clerks shaking his head in disbelief. Worse, the Hound knew this clerk from his hockey team.

The Hound tried to make light of it, but he knew, and his hockey friend knew, he was guilty of something. He had heard about the ring theft—and now, this?

The Hound knew the whole town would hear about it.

104

How Many More Times

He appeared before the judge, who was going to book a hearing. The judge said, "Due to the nature of the charge, I do not want you around the kids at home. So you have a protection order. You are not to be within one mile of your home."

The Hound called Marie and asked her to bring him some of his stuff. He had a new place to stay, the beach.

Marie brought him some things and decided to have a heart to heart. "You have to make a choice," she told him. "You have to decide between the beer and your beautiful new son, Max."

The Hound looked at her and he knew the lie was over. He could no longer make her believe that he could be a good father and husband and still drink everyday. His stomach tightened like a ball, and he pushed the feeling back down his throat as he mumbled the answer. To him, it was obvious.

"I choose the beer."

He tried to imagine his life without drinking. That was scarier than death. The drink was his best friend. It filled the emptiness within him. It was the only thing that ever worked. For as long as he could remember, it was always there for him. It didn't judge him, it only comforted him. How could he give that up? So even though he loved his son, to the Hound, there was no choice.

Marie left.

105

In The Flesh

The Hound took up residence at the beach and spent most of his evenings at the bar. He was still seal coating and getting cash to support his bad habits.

One night, he snuck home to visit Marie after the kids had gone to sleep. He was drunk, so it was easy to ignore the fact that he wasn't supposed to be there.

Marie was annoyed. The Hound couldn't believe she was not happy to see him. Marie was his last person on Earth that still loved him. Her being annoyed with him was a threat to the last vestiges of good within him. Losing his temper, he threw her into the closet before escaping himself into the bathroom and locking the door.

Trapped within this small space, full of self loathing, not wanting to see the wreckage he had created and close to insane, he needed to do something desperately. *I'll show her how crazy I am!* he thought. Taking his clothes off, and running a bath, he thought of taking his own life. Opening the drawer and grabbing all of the Bic razors that Marie had, he climbed into the warm water. Instead of trying to cut his wrists, he decided he'd start by shaving his whole body - including his eyebrows. He wanted to look like Pink from *The Wall.*

He staggered out of the tub and ventured back into the bedroom. Marie had gone. Bleeding from a hundred razor cuts, the Hound passed out on the bed.

When he woke up, he tried to throw the sheet off him. To his surprise, the blood had congealed with the sheet and stuck to him in a hundred different places. He had to walk into the shower with the sheet and use the hot water to peel the material from his skin.

Marie came up with a coffee, and finally drew the line in the sand.

"I love you, honey. But I can't live like this anymore."

For the first time in their life, the Hound knew she meant it. No amount of charm, no funny antidotes, no promises of babies or new houses or fresh starts were going to work this time. She was done.

It was over.

106

Love Reign O'er Me

The Hound got dressed that morning, as the north wind blew through his soul.

He knew for sure he was alone.

Back to the beach, back to seal-coating. The Hound drank around the clock now. He couldn't bear a minute of sobriety, as his self-pity and self-loathing and loneliness were unbearable.

One night he decided to go to the nightclub and he was already too drunk to walk straight. As he made his way through the crowd, trying to find some lonely girl to connect with, the music pounded out and the crowds parted like the Red Sea as he staggered towards people. He lost his balance and went out the front door, landing on the sidewalk.

The dry ice from the nightclub followed behind him, and the music became muffled as the door closed.

He tried to get up, but he couldn't.

The world spun beneath him and he heard the laughter of the people who looked down on him. He realized at that moment. *I'm just a drunk. A common street drunk. A hobo laying on the ground and I can't get up. I'm a loser after all.*

This was his first admission to himself of his powerlessness.

107

Asylum

He appeared before a judge for his theft charge. "Theft Above a Thousand Dollars" was the official crime. The judge regarded him curiously.

"What is your problem?" The judge asked. "You were in good standing in the community, held an important job, had a family, and now you are in front of me for a criminal charge. How do you explain that?"

The Hound had no explanation. "I don't know, Your Honor, I had a bad year."

The judge decided he needed a professional opinion. He decided to find him guilty of the charge, fine him, but his sentencing would be determined after the Hound went to a psychologist for evaluation.

The Hound went unenthusiastically. He'd been down this road before.

The psychologist didn't take long to determine the Hound was an alcoholic.

The Hound thought this was the stupidest thing he ever heard. Of course he was an alcoholic. He *loved* alcohol. This was no revelation. He just didn't imagine he could ever change it.

"There's a place," said the psychologist, "where they treat this sort of thing. If I make a recommendation to the judge, are you willing to go? I don't see how going to jail *again* will help you, but this might."

The Hound thought for a second. *Jail or the Country Club?* "Sure," he said. "I'll go."

108

Surrender

The Hound called Marie and explained the situation. They had sold their house, had a little bit of money left after the mortgage and the bills had been paid.

Marie agreed she'd drive him to the treatment center. If he was willing to change, she'd give him one more chance.

The other charges were dropped, as the women had a change of heart. One less thing looming over him. He dodged the bullet on that one.

They bought an old Pontiac station wagon. It was burgundy, with wooden panels on all sides of the car. "A Woody Wagon" they called it. It was huge, and fit all the kids and all their belongings.

They made the three hour drive to the coast, and pulled into the treatment center. The Hound was nervous, he didn't really want to go in there.

They had moved from the town where all his shame was. He didn't need treatment—he just needed a fresh start. He tried to convince Marie, but she had come all this way, and she didn't trust him. "Why don't you just go in and give it a chance?" she said, "I'll be here when you get out."

He knew she wasn't going to let him come with her. So he gave her a hug, and a kiss goodbye and she left. Marie went over to a campsite nearby, to live in a tent for the month, with her two kids and the baby.

She was terrified that this treatment center wasn't going to work. She also had her doubts that the Hound would stay there for the whole 28 days. She fully expected to get a drunken phone call from him that he had run away and was in some pub.

As she pulled out of the parking lot, the Hound looked up the stairs to the door of the center, and panic set in. *I'll make a run for it*, he thought. *I'll go down the street, to the pub, I got enough money to get drunk.*

But he hung his head and knew that meant nobody would ever love him again. This was the last house on the block. If he walked past this door, he would live in the darkness on the edge of town forever. He had one last chance at a life with Marie and the kids. A family. Love. Meaning. Purpose. Up the stairs there was still a glimmer of hope that he could have the life that he knew he would never have, if he took a drink. So, he mustered all the strength he could and walked into the treatment center. *Get well, or live in Hell.*

If he took that drink, what awaited him was the company of strangers, other alcoholics, prostitutes, policemen, prisons, and Satan himself.

109

People Are Strange

The Hound was assigned his room, and went in and met his roomate. His name was John. A middle aged guy, his wife had sent him to the treatment center. He didn't seem like he had been through that much yet. The Hound prejudged him as a lightweight, but a friendly enough roommate.

They both walked down to the meeting room to meet the counselors and the other patients.

The Hound took a chair at the back of the room—an old habit. *Keep everybody in front of you—that way you can keep an eye on 'em.*

There was a mixture of people alright: old and young, short and tall, well groomed and toothless. Looked like alcohol had no prejudice.

The counselors introduced themselves and began by welcoming the participants. They explained that they were going to get some "education" on the disease of alcoholism. After lunch they would break into smaller groups to start to get to know each other.

The counselor explained the different types of alcoholics. There was the A type, a maintenance drinker, and the B type, a binge drinker. The maintenance drinker drank every day, but was able to function without anyone knowing. She could be a professional, or he might be a mechanic.

The B type, the "Jekyll and Hyde"—this was the Hound. He recognized himself in this description. Normal nice guy one day, add alcohol—instant werewolf. *Awoooo!*

As they went on that morning explaining all the history and medical knowledge, the genetic disposition and the clinical trials, the Hound was fascinated. All this time he thought he was unique—that only he suffered this strange obsession; to drink something that would send him into a black out with all sorts of antisocial behavior. To pour that poison into him, knowing the wreckage that was coming, to the furniture and the family.

He never understood why but he was starting to see that he wasn't alone; if this behavior was so textbook, then maybe, just maybe, they would have a cure.

The food at lunch that day tasted better than food had tasted in a long time. The orange juice looked so orange, and the apple was so red. He was starting to become grateful to be alive.

That afternoon they broke up into smaller groups and met their psychologist. It was group therapy—but they didn't call it that.

The Hound took his chair in the corner, back against the wall and prepared for the mental gymnastics.

He looked around the room; sizing everybody up. He was the best looking one, and probably the smartest—he thought; *I wonder what all these losers are gonna talk about.*

One guy said he wasn't really an alcoholic. He was just there because his boss made him come. They all knew he was lying. The Hound wondered how many sessions it would take for him to realize it.

One girl talked about sleeping with everybody. The Hound related to her. He wondered if he would end up sleeping with her before he got out of there.

The Hound grinned to himself and thought, *You sick bastard...you're supposed to be getting better in here.*

Another guy, an old fart, looked like his fight with alcohol was past recovery, as he looked like he might die that week.

The Hound felt himself getting more cynical and cracking jokes. This was his defense system against getting in touch with his own emotions.

When it was his turn, he switched on the charm. With a big smile, the Hound answered all the questions with witty answers and funny comments.

The psychologist understood the Hound was deflecting.

The Hound managed to protect whatever secret he thought he needed to hide. He had no intention of exposing his inner self to these losers. He must hide his true feelings, which wasn't hard, because he didn't know what they were. *Just keep them laughing, and they'll leave me alone.*

110

Runnin' Down A Dream

Back at the recovery center, the Hound did some reading and writing. He was trying to figure this thing out *fast*, so that he could get out of there.

He thought, *If it takes these morons a month to get this, I should be able to figure it out in a week.*

The Hound started to get up early and run every morning. He'd head down over the bridge, into the park and run along next to the ducks floating in the lake; under the tree cover, and across the grass. It was just a few miles—but it felt so good, to feel his legs working again. To breathe in the fresh air, and make his heart pound.

His sweat was finally alcohol-free.

As he headed back, he'd break into a sprint the last hundred yards.

The Hound loved to run at full speed.

At top speed, he felt superhuman. Like a running animal he felt every muscle and ounce of strength in his body; as powerful as a train, and as nimble as a cat—a big cat.

In this moment he felt true joy—all thought was gone, all doubt, all fear. It was just him, riding this body, like a horse, with the wind in his hair, and everything a blur. He was winning the race.

How could he not control a stupid drink? How could this magnificent intelligent powerful specimen not just be able to use his willpower to not drink anymore? It didn't make any sense. He thought he'd call Marie and tell her to come pick him up—after all he'd been there three days.

How could he be powerless?

111

Breakdown

Marie had no home, and in those days it meant she had no phone. The Hound didn't even know where she was, some campsite somewhere, so he was not going to leave. He'd already paid, and the food was pretty good, and he had nowhere to go.

The Hound knew, at some level, that nothing had really changed yet; that he needed to stay and dig deeper.

After a few weeks everybody in the group had broken down: the guy in denial admitted his alcoholism and had a good cry. They all encouraged him. The horny girl talked about how her father didn't love her, and so she was looking for male validation. And the old guy regretted that it had taken him so long to get there, but it was never too late for a fresh start. The Hound admired his self delusion.

So far the Hound had danced his way around his own heart, cleverly redirecting the counselor's questions, averting any real emotion.

The counselor was very clever, and needed a strategy to fool the Hound. So the next time the Hound began to answer with a smile and glib response, the counselor stopped him. "You are a very good salesman, aren't you?"

"Well, yeah, I'm pretty good," the Hound faked humility.

"I see that," said the counselor. "Problem is, I can't really take the salesman seriously. So, are you willing to try something new with me?"

"Sure," said the Hound, overconfident.

"Okay," said the counselor. "The next time you start to answer a question, and you stay in that seat, I will understand that it's *salesman* answering me. But—if you want to tell me the answer from *you*, I want you to move to the empty chair next to you, and answer from there."

The Hound laughed at this silly proposition. "No problem."

The counselor moved off to another patient, and discussed some issues with them.

The Hound felt abandoned. *Hey, I thought it was my turn,* thought the Hound.

Soon enough, the counselor came back to him. He already knew some of the Hound's story. Even the fateful day when he had dropped the ball in front of his father, but the Hound had laughed it off, making a joke about his feelings.

The counselor suspected that this was much more of a

big deal than the Hound was letting on. He asked the Hound, "Tell me again how you felt, when you looked up and saw your father leaving that day at the championship game."

Just as the Hound was about to answer, the counselor stopped him and asked, "Is this the salesman answering?"

The Hound laughed. "Oh yeah!" and he then moved to the empty chair. As soon as the weight of his body sank into the chair, he tried to speak, but couldn't. His stomach flexed, and he squeezed his fists, trying to not let the feelings come up his throat.

He gritted his teeth and started to shudder as the dam of emotions exploded through. He fought and fought but it was no use. He was overcome by shame and grief and anger and self-loathing, and he wept and screamed. Snot fell from his nose, and he drooled out his mouth as he buried his face in his hands and wept at the lonely and unlovable creature he was.

112

A Long Time Running

The relief was exhilarating as he gathered himself, wiping his eyes and blowing his nose. He felt like a thousand pounds had been lifted off his heart; that the elephant that was sitting on his chest had finally gone.

He remembered his Shakespeare; *Whether 'tis nobler in the mind to suffer the slings and arrows of outrageous fortune,* but this time the Hound remembered the rest of the soliloquy: *...or to take arms against a sea of troubles, and by opposing end them?*

He knew now, if he wanted to recover, he'd have to stop running and turn and face his sea of troubles.

He had finally faced his dragon, and feeling his feelings was the only way past it.

He now understood he'd been running all this time.

And like *the Warriors* from Coney Island, he only stopped running because he was exhausted. So he turned to face it.

The counselor knew this was a huge breakthrough, that the Hound had been drinking at himself for his failure to live up to what he thought his father wanted, and that all the Hound really needed was acceptance and praise and love.

So the counselor told the Hound, "You did great. That was really good work."

The Hound didn't know how to feel, hearing this praise. He liked it, but was uncomfortable still.

Then the counselor doubled down and asked if anybody else had anything to tell the Hound. The old man squinted his eyes like a cowboy and said, "That took some gumption, I saw you fighting and I felt your struggle. Congrats."

The Hound's head was spinning. He didn't know what to do with all this praise. He still felt embarrassed for breaking down in front of them all.

As the horny girl was looking at the Hound, she said, "I didn't think you were brave enough to get there."

The denial guy said, "You've been in some denial of your own. Welcome back to the real world."

The Hound was so uncomfortable with all this praise, that he got up and sat back in the salesman's chair. *Safe at last!*

113

More Than A Feeling

The Hound had a newfound respect for the counselor. He really didn't see it coming and he was grateful that he had been outsmarted. He really thought he was finished with the treatment now. After all, what else could he need? He finally found self-forgiveness, and he pinned down the traumatic event that started this whole journey of alcoholism. So... he should be good to go, eh?

After a few more days the cynicism returned to the Hound. The pink cloud had worn off, he felt irritable, restless, and discontent. His skin started to crawl again and he started to pick on other people, just verbally. He had an edge to him, an edge that could cut.

He thought that he'd be cured by his revelation, but all that it had offered him was some temporary relief. Alas, here he was again, uncomfortable in his own skin.

His mind raced ahead, to Marie and the kids, and work,

and how he was wasting his time sitting in this place—that none of this was going to help him make a living.

This wasn't going to take away his depression or his anxiety. He was disappointed and he asked the counselor if he could see him one on one.

He explained to the counselor that he was grateful for the breakthrough he had helped him with, but that the black dog was back on him again. That he was depressed again, and he had little hope of surviving on the outside without a drink.

The counselor was delighted to hear this. "I'm so glad you understand that there is no quick fix; that this is a lifetime affliction. That only a very small percentage of people get well. This treatment center is only an awakening. If you have any hope at all of staying sober, you're gonna need ongoing support; a program you can live, a fellowship to belong to, and a higher power to help you."

"Well I don't believe in God," said the Hound. "That's for suckers and weak minded people. For losers that had to believe in some imaginary deity. Believing he would solve all their problems and are so desperate they're willing to get ripped off by some TV evangelist."

"Well," said the counselor, "you don't have to believe in all that, but I strongly encourage you to keep an open mind, and I want you to go with us tonight to an AA meeting."

"Fuck that!" said the Hound. "That's a cult! I'll never believe in all that bullshit."

"Well, I want you to look at your resistance, and ask yourself, if it's all bullshit, why am I so against even looking—shouldn't I go first, before I make up my mind?"

The Hound felt indebted to him for the breakthrough the counselor helped him with, so although he had no faith whatsoever, he agreed to check it out.

That night the Hound showed up to the meeting and took the chair at the back of the room. His arms were folded, and his cynicism was at full alert. He was ready to reject this dogma at first glance.

114

Reason to Believe

Alcoholics Anonymous sounded like *The Freemasons* or *The Rotary Club,* some boring do-gooder outfit.

The Hound looked around the room, but couldn't find anything to hang his hat on, yet. He was looking for some fatal flaw, some reason he could condemn the whole thing.

They started the meeting and they broke into a prayer. The Hound didn't pray. *That was for weirdos.*

They started talking about the steps, and that it was the steps that were the way to freedom and that the steps were "the answer" to long term sobriety.

The Hound understood that this was the counselor's only answer after treatment. That this was the *last house on the block.* That if he couldn't grasp and accept the principles of AA, then he had no chance of staying sober.

The Hound was desperate, as desperate as the dying can

be. He wanted these steps to work. He knew that drinking again would mean the loss of Marie, the loss of Max, Jessica and Marcus, and his ability to work, play sports, pay bills, have a home, or even to stay alive.

He knew where the drink would take him. It would take him to needing more, it would take him to do anything to get more, and even when he got more, he would be left empty, begging for oblivion. That life would have no meaning except misery, casual conversations amongst the walking dead. There would be no intimacy, no joy, no hope.

He looked up at the Twelve Steps written in large print hanging from two posters on the wall behind the person leading the meeting. They looked like the Ten Commandments, and he hoped there was some logic in them, something he could get his brain wrapped around, something that would give him a calculated path to freedom.

He read the first step. "We admitted we were powerless over alcohol—that our lives had become unmanageable."

In light of all the wreckage that drinking had caused him, and all the damage he had done to his family, his standing in the community and his self esteem, he could accept this step.

Step 2: "Came to believe that a Power greater than ourselves could restore us to sanity."

There it was: "A Power greater than ourselves." *This was just code for God.* The Hound was starting to get defensive.

The meeting had started, and people were talking, but the Hound wasn't listening. He was doing his own investigation.

Step 3: "Made a decision to turn our will and our lives over to the care of God as we understood Him."

Bang! There it was. To his horror, he saw the word *God.* First it was written as a "Power greater than yourself." Then, there it was, in plain sight, by step 3. *He was in the Catholic church.*

What's next? Communion and Baptism? And some bullshit about a virgin?

Step 4: "Made a searching and fearless moral inventory of ourselves.

Step 5: "Admitted to God, to ourselves, and to another human being the exact nature of our wrongs."

Here we go. God again! And now they wanted him to go to confession.

Step 6: "Were entirely ready to have God remove all these defects of character."

The Hound didn't need to read any more steps. The flicker of hope that still burned deep in his heart, was blown out. God was the answer in here, and God wouldn't work for the Hound. It couldn't work. It required a lobotomy, a removal of all common sense, any scientific thinking, any logic—any rational view of the human condition.

The Hound knew there and then he would die an alcoholic.

115

I Saw The Light

The Hound got up, and hung his head as he watched his feet shuffle out of the meeting. He didn't notice anybody, and he couldn't hear anything either.

He went outside of the meeting, turned the corner on the terrace, and sat down on the steps. It was dark, nobody was there and it was at this moment that he said to himself, "I'm a dead man. I have no chance of recovery." He wondered how he was going to explain this to Marie. He wondered how long he could fake his recovery, how many more lies he could tell. He knew deep down in his heart that only misery and failure lay ahead. He wondered at that moment if he could will himself to die.

He slumped back against the step, in complete defeat. It was the darkest moment of his life.

All hope was gone.

No sooner had he completely given up, a bright light appeared before him: it was a translucent figure. The man opened his arms with his hands out to the side, like he was welcoming the Hound home, and said only one thing:

"Believe in me and all will be well."

116

Bridge Over Troubled Water

As quick as the figure came, He was gone.

The light was out.

But something remained, something deep inside the Hound's soul.

The Hound took a breath and wondered if what happened was real or imagined. He didn't know for sure, but something had changed inside him. He now felt a mustard seed of hope.

He got up and walked back into the meeting. He sat down and, for the first time in his life, he began to hear.

The first thing the Hound noticed was that he wasn't as suspicious or cynical any more.

He started to understand the words that were being said; that everybody in there was on the same boat.

He heard someone say in the meeting that God could be "whatever you wanted it to be"—it could stand, for example, for "Good Orderly Direction" or the group *itself*. One lady called God, "Group Of Drunks."

Another, older fellow said his God was the "Great Out Doors." That the higher power was called God, not for dogma, but just to describe something that might be able to help the drunk get sober. A way to fill the vacancy inside with something other than the vice of booze.

The people relating stories were honest, revealing some of their biggest fears and worst embarrassments. The Hound never heard people talk like this before. Most times in life, people were bragging about who they were and what they've accomplished in life. *That wasn't the vibe in this room.*

Everybody was self-effacing, not in a pitiful way—just more matter-of-fact. And they all went on to explain it was the attendance of AA meetings and the working of the *Twelve Steps* that brought them recovery.

The Hound didn't speak in that meeting but for the first time in his life he didn't feel alone any more.

117

Suspicious Minds

It was his last week in the treatment center and Marie came in for couples counseling.

The Hound was so happy to see her. She looked beautiful to him; more beautiful than anything in the world. He raced over to her and embraced her. They held each other for a long time. The Hound felt like he could breathe again. That he had come up from the depths of a dark ocean, and finally broke the surface to feel the sunlight and breathe the air.

Marie seemed happy, she loved the Hound.

He explained to her that he had some major breakthroughs in therapy, and that he even went to an AA meeting, although he wasn't completely sold on it yet.

She wasn't sold on the idea of her needing counseling. After all—the Hound had the problem, not her.

The counselors tried to have her see that maybe she was enabling him by allowing him to get away with things. They tried to stress to her that she had to set boundaries and hold him accountable.

This all sounded good in theory, but Marie knew the Hound was not easily controlled and she didn't think he was that bad anyway.

She had an innate way of accepting everything and not judging people. She believed people were flawed, and that a good drink wouldn't hurt anyone. She wasn't naive—Marie understood the Hound could be dangerous—but she saw something in him, something that inexplicably bound her to him. Marie wasn't one to apologize for things that belonged to her.

She was willing to support the Hound, but it was clear early on that she wasn't going to take part in any psychobabble about her. She would be there for him on the other side of the bridge. But Marie knew there was no bridge for her to cross.

Recovery was on the Hound…and the Hound alone. Marie didn't need it, thank you very much.

118

Proud Mary

It was graduation day from the treatment center, and the Hound was very grateful to the counselor for helping him have his breakthrough. The Hound believed that he was cured from alcoholism. He explained to Marie again that he owed it all to this counselor, gave him a big hug, and said goodbye.

The counselor cautioned him. "Remember, you *need* the AA meetings if you're going to make it."

The Hound thanked all the people in the center. He really felt like he had a fresh start. At the very least, he'd shown Marie he was serious.

He said his goodbyes, and they headed back to the campsite.

The kids gave him a mixed reception. Marcus let him hug him, but didn't hug him back. He wasn't too thrilled about having to live in a tent. As far as Marcus could see, it was all the Hound's fault.

Jessica came over to give him a hug, but it was quick, and not too sincere.

The baby seemed happy to see him, but he couldn't speak yet. The Hound picked Max up and hugged him with deep love and reverence.

Marie cracked open a beer. The Hound was slightly offended. "What are you doing?" he asked.

"I'm having a beer," she said. "I'm not the drunk here."

The Hound was in no position to disagree. Marie was setting the ground rules early. She was going to have her drink when she wanted it. After all, she usually only had one. She wasn't going to hide it, she wasn't going to tiptoe around him. If he wanted to quit, he'd have to be able to handle being around it.

119

Telegraph Road

It was time to find a new town. Time to find a house and try to make it a home. Time to get a job and get the kids in school, so that they could get on with their life.

They really didn't have much money. Marie found a home in a small remote town. It was for sale for only 29,000 dollars. She knew they had enough for a downpayment on that one. So they packed up and headed up there.

After a long drive, they came down out of the mountains. It was raining in that small remote town. The realtor showed them the house. It was pretty beat up: a three story with tiny rooms and lots of staircases. It looked like it had been built during the first World War.

It had to be close to a hundred years old. It had a wood fireplace in the basement, and the chimney ran up right through the middle of the house. It was a cheap way to get heat in the winter but the fireplace was leaking kerosene.

Black oil was oozing through the bricks.

The Hound was full of positivity; it didn't deter him. "This will be perfect!" he said, and they bought the house.

The Hound took a sledgehammer to the chimney as the kids were picking their rooms, Marie was making something to eat in the kitchen, so the Hound tackled removing the chimney by himself. It was a huge job, but once the Hound set his mind to something, he was a maniac.

A week or ten days later he had the whole thing in a pile in the backyard. Now they needed to hire a carpenter to close the holes in the floors and ceilings. He let Marie handle that as he drove the old Pontiac down to the Toyota store to see if he could get a job.

They weren't hiring in the main store, but they had a small used car lot down by the factory. The owner told him he could go work there.

The car lot only had ten cars on it, none of them very new. The asphalt had cracks in it, with weeds growing up through it. The building looked like an old gas station, with a flat roof, single-pane glass for walls. Perfect if you'd like to stare out at the smoke billowing out of the factory and watch the rain endlessly fall from the dark sky.

He went inside and noticed it had old bad carpeting and two unmatching desks with ugly chairs. At one of the desks sat an old bearded guy. "My name is Wyatt," he said.

He had no mustache, just a beard and looked like an Amish elder. His hair was gray and he was heavy set, a large man, with a kind face.

The Hound didn't know it, but this was a gift from God, for Wyatt was a man of faith, and understood the frailties of human behavior.

He and the Hound would talk for hours. The Hound had a lot to learn.

The factory across the street was a pulp mill, he recognized the smell from the town up north. When the cloud cover was heavy, and the rain poured, it trapped the smell in the valley.

It rained for sixty days straight that winter. They had moved to the wettest town in the world. There was a reason the houses were so cheap. The town bordered an inlet on the Pacific Ocean, and was surrounded by mountains. The ocean storms would blow heavy rains up the inlet and when the clouds hit the mountains they emptied the entire rainstorm on top of the Hound.

They'd only get one or two customers a day. He and Wyatt took turns. The Hound soon realized he'd need another job as well. Straight commission on three cars a month wasn't going to cut it.

He got a job driving taxi. He had never drove taxi before. After all, he was a college graduate, and a manager of car dealerships. *How had he ended up here?*

Picking up old ladies from the bingo hall and driving them home through the rain at ten o'clock at night. He was intimidated by the voices that came across the CB radio. They were other cabbies and the dispatcher. They had a language of their own, and the Hound didn't speak it.

He didn't dare enter into the banter, for he knew he

wasn't one of them. They were blue collar people, working people—good people, but different from the Hound. At least he thought so.

One night, he took a fellow back to the reserve, and when he dropped him off, the man told him "I have no money. But you can drink some beer with me."

The Hound was feeling pretty depressed and thought hard about drinking the beer the man had offered. But he managed to decline and told him it was okay, he didn't have to pay.

The Hound drove away, and only had two other fares that night. So when he returned the car to the dispatcher, he had worked an eight-hour shift, and only made about three dollars.

He quit that night. He went home to Marie, had dinner. As he put Max to bed he stroked his face with the back of his hand, and as he tucked the blanket in under his chin, he whispered, "Don't worry, son, we'll make it somehow."

120

New Kid In Town

The next night the Hound went to his first AA meeting in town. It was a close call last night, and he thought he'd better shore himself up.

He pulled the pontiac into the parking lot and nervously made his way to the door. It was in a back room of the library. He peeked in and saw eight or ten people. He was so nervous he didn't notice anything about them.

"Welcome," they said, "come on in, sit down."

The Hound sat down uncomfortably. Somebody started the meeting. It didn't look like they were in charge of anything, but they led the others through the readings and the steps.

He managed to sit through it, and didn't really get much out of it. People were saying weird things that he didn't understand, things about faith and "surrendering."

Soon the meeting was ending—*not soon enough*. They were all holding hands and were saying a prayer. The Hound almost left, he wasn't much for holding hands with strangers, let alone prayer.

All the Hound knew was hard work and self will. He thought most of these people must have failed at life to end up here. He felt sorry for them: broken down losers huddling together in the dark, holding hands and praying to some imaginary god to come save them. *Pathetic.*

After the meeting was over some guy introduced himself to the Hound and told him that he'd be his sponsor. The Hound said, "Okay," not really understanding what that was, and the guy hugged him.

The Hound never went back to this meeting again, for fear of the hugger.

121

The End

With AA being of no use, the Hound soon was irritable, restless and discontent again: the kids never picked their shit up, and Marie paid too much attention to little Max; supper wasn't ready on time, and she was spending too much money.

Inevitably the Hound blamed her for everything.

If only he didn't have to deal with all this crap he'd be able to succeed. *They weren't well matched,* he thought. *It was time to get out on his own.*

The Hound told her he was going to leave her.

Marie said, "Good riddance!" She had about enough of his bad mood.

The Hound found a room above a bar. It was up a narrow staircase and down a hall with three or four rooms; his room was number four. As he opened the door it looked like a 1975 travel trailer. It had lime green counters, an orange shag rug and plastic furniture. It only had one window, an old couch and a bed in the corner.

The Hound dropped his bag of clothes, putting his toothbrush in the bathroom. *Free at last. Free at last! Thank God, I'm free at last!*

He headed downstairs and ordered a beer.

He drank five or six, as fast as he could, and sized up the women in the bar. Nobody was paying any attention to him, they were already preoccupied with whoever they were with. So he bought a twelve pack and went back to his room.

Four or five beers later he decided it was a town full of losers, and he was pulling outta here to win. *Again.*

He checked out of the room, and with the family car he escaped to the city.

An old friend was having a party, so the Hound got a case of beer and showed up. He tried socializing, but he couldn't do small talk well; they all seemed fake to him. He just wanted to get wasted.

He bought some cocaine off someone, and decided to call a limousine service. He wanted to party in style. He might be socially awkward but he would remedy that with grandiosity. The limousine and some cocaine and he would feel like the king of the world.

When the limo driver came, the Hound piled in the back seat with his case of beer, a bag of cocaine and a bottle of champagne he stole from the party. He told the driver he'd give him a few hundred bucks and some cocaine if he would party with him until the sun came up. The driver calculated it was probably his last fare anyway, so he agreed.

The Hound told him to go and get a hooker. The limo driver knew just where to go, and soon enough they had a rolling party. They drank, snorted and screwed around till the sun came up and the hooker had gone. The Hound was drinking the last of the champagne straight from the bottle.

He sat in the back seat of the limo with the window down, watching the sun come up and listening to the birds laughing at him.

He knew that he had fucked up, that he had thrown away the only thing that had meant anything to him: Marie and the kids. Once again he was fooled by the devil; to chase some elusive high that made him feel better than everybody else, above it all, a winner, a king—but in the end it was an illusion. In reality, it only delivered him sorrow, loneliness and failure; he wasn't winning, he was an all-time loser. No idea how to live life, and no ability to connect with anybody. An insatiable vacuum, that could never fill the emptiness within him. That's all he was.

He had the taste of blood in his mouth, and had drunk himself sober. Self loathing and demoralization laid on him like a blanket. Once again, he wished for death.

122

Don't Stop Believin'

He knew he had to go back to Marie and beg for her forgiveness and redouble his efforts at sobriety, he had to look after the kids, and pay the bills. *He needed to try harder.*

On his way back home he stopped at the jewelry store and bought Marie an engagement ring. This time he paid for it, he put it on his credit card, he had just enough room to cover the ring.

He pulled into the driveway, anxious that she might reject him. But when he got on one knee and gave her the ring, her heart melted and she took him back.

He was so relieved. Out there it was so lonely and scary. He got strength from his family and with Marie by his side, he still had a fighting chance.

During dinner that night he told her, "I think there's more to me than this, Marie. I have to go to the other side of the island and get a real job. I can manage a real dealership again. I have to try."

Marie was supportive, but not enthusiastic. "If that's what you want to do, you should do it."

"Don't give up on me yet," said the Hound, "I'll make you proud."

123

Low Budget

It was an hour's drive over the mountain back to the big city. The Hound pulled into the first dealership he saw and met the man that was going to be his new boss.

Roy was a short man with a robust and red complexion, who talked through his nose. He asked the Hound about his background and was impressed to learn that he had managed a Toyota dealership.

"But," the Hound said, "I have to be honest with you. I left in a disgrace. I am an alcoholic. But I went to treatment and I'm sober now. So I'll be the best version of myself."

Roy liked the Hound. "Okay bud," he said with his nasal voice, seeing an opportunity to underpay the Hound. "I'll give you the job, but I'm only paying ya $3,750 a month."

It was a low offer, but a lot better than how he'd been living. So he took the job. He got a new car for a demo, a

Saab 900, and sped back across the mountains to tell Marie the good news.

Marie was excited for him, but she wasn't going to move the kids during the school year, so the Hound made the hour drive back and forth every day.

The Hound knew that he needed to try the AA meetings again. The pressures of a new job would be hard on him. He didn't want to start drinking again, that would ruin everything. He had to get committed to his recovery.

He found a new AA meeting close to work. This group seemed a lot more normal—but damn old. He was the youngest one in the room by far, but they were friendly and nobody tried to hug him.

124

With Or Without You

Several months went by and they were getting their bills paid. Things were going well. One night, Marie and the Hound tuned into the local small-town radio station and heard the announcement that the Hound had won the scoring championship in the men's hockey league.

It felt like being eight years old again. He was getting sober, and God had let him win the title.

He didn't really believe in God, though he was *trying*. He wanted to want to believe.

The Hound was okay with believing that God had rewarded him for *good* behavior, that if he worked hard towards something he was good at, God might bless him with a victory.

That was the extent of it, as faith didn't translate to his everyday life. He didn't use God for anything else; the

Hound didn't pray in the morning, he had yet to understand that God might be able to affect his thinking or his behavior. He was still spiritually void and his philosophy was still self-reliance. He had no faith.

This was a recipe for disaster.

The Hound expected the kids to behave the way he thought they should; for work to go as he saw fit; people to listen to him about every detail that his perfectionist mind pointed out. He saw how the world *should* be, and when it wasn't—it would infuriate him.

One day, he turned his obsessive mind toward Marie again. It had been a long day at work, and when the Hound got home, he expected a meal. The kids weren't disciplined properly, and the house was a mess. *After all, Marie wasn't even working!*

The Hound exploded in a rage. "What the fuck? Why can't you just keep the house clean, the kids in order, and have a meal ready for me when I get home?"

Marie snapped back. "The world doesn't revolve around you!"

This sent the Hound off the deep end. *The disrespect! Who did she think she was talking to?*

He was the man. *He* was putting a roof over her head and feeding her kids.

His self righteous anger was out of control. He wanted to smash her head off the wall and put her in her place. He wanted to teach her who was boss.

Just before carrying out this violence, the Hound instinctively knew he had to run. Grabbing the car keys, he headed out the front door. He backed the car out of the driveway, and squealed the tires as he sped off down the road.

The Hound smashed the palm of his hand against the steering wheel, gripping it with both hands and let out a scream. "FUCK YOU!"

He ran a stop sign and took a corner too fast as the car swerved down the road. The Hound was heading to the bar.

He *had* to get a drink.

125

Suzanne

He had no defense against the first drink.

As tears streamed down his face, the Hound knew that he shouldn't take a drink; as it would only end in more misery, and he would lose his family and ultimately, his will to live.

In a blind panic he turned towards a Texaco gas station and parked the car. His breath was rapid and his skin crawled. The Hound knew that this maneuver of pulling into the gas station would only delay the inevitable.

He didn't need gas, so the Hound ran inside to get the bathroom key. He didn't need to go to the bathroom either, but the Hound needed a place to hide.

Once safely inside the bathroom, he locked the door and flipped on the light as he sat on top of the toilet seat. The Hound was vibrating, still so angry at Marie, he couldn't get past his resentment, yet he had no idea how to deal with these feelings, and this urge to drink them away.

In an act of desperation, like a drowning man, he called out to God. "If you exist, then help me. Help me not take a drink."

His head fell into his hands and he closed his eyes tight, as a sense of calmness came over him—

Something changed.

His paradigm shifted. The Hound surveyed the bathroom stall, at the graffiti and the scribbled penises drawn on the walls, the used up toilet paper scattered across the floor, the urine that missed its aim, and the smell of an unkept bathroom.

He began to laugh.

Laughing at the irony, the Hound realized God had just answered his prayer in a Texaco toilet.

He glanced around and realized that if he was laughing at himself, he didn't need to take a drink. That God had done for him what he couldn't do for himself. He just needed to ask.

The Hound was drowning alright, engulfed in his self centeredness. He struggled with his self-pity and false pride, expecting the world to cater to his needs. The Hound was sinking because he had no idea how to swim.

Standing up and brushing himself off, he had another chuckle at the ridiculousness of this scene, and knew just what he had to do.

The Hound had to go home and apologize to Marie. *Again.*

126

Let 'Em In

This was the first time in the Hound's life that when the obsession to drink had overtaken him, that he had managed to avoid drunkenness.

This was a miracle.

Not as dramatic as turning water into wine or healing a leper, but, to him it was just as miraculous.

He had asked God to take away the desire for the drink, and he had been given reprieve. Humor had helped him break the spell. The Hound now knew that no matter how rudimentary his faith was, that there was something to it. That somehow it had worked.

Ask and you shall receive.

127

The Lonely End Of The Rink

It was time to move to the big city. The Hound found a great family home. The kids would each get their own room, mom and dad had the whole upstairs to themselves. It was a big Tudor-style house, with a large brick fireplace in the living room and a galley kitchen.

It had a plush, deep green rug, a dark wood staircase, a small backyard, and was surrounded by trees. There was a garden on the side of the house, and a wide, flat driveway.

The whole family was thrilled and with the Hound's new job and new car, from the outside they looked like a perfect family.

Behind the walls still roamed an untreated alcoholic and a family walking on eggshells.

The Hound could be so kind and loving, wrestling with the children and playing rug hockey—a game he taught the children where they would crumple up tinfoil into a ball and use it as a hockey puck as they lay on the rug. They pretended to be NHL stars as they shot the tinfoil ball at each other and made great saves.

The Hound was a good provider. They always had food and clothing and Marie was the emotional rock.

When the Hound would lose his temper, it wasn't pretty. Many times he'd drive his car down to the end of the block, stop and say his prayer, and then head home with his tail between his legs to apologize again. He hated this cycle of losing control of his emotions, running away to nowhere. Then only to have to return, embarrassed and ashamed, to beg for forgiveness.

The Hound would go to one AA meeting a week, it was Tuesday night, seven o'clock. He met an old fellow there named John.

John was seventy-seven years old and had been sober for seven years. The Hound thought this was amazing to get sober at *that* age.

John was a kind man, and when the Hound missed the Tuesday night meeting, the phone would ring. The Hound would answer it, usually in some disturbed state of mind, and the soft old voice would come through the phone, "We missed you at the meeting tonight."

The Hound didn't know whether to be offended by the intrusion or touched by the concern. "Yeah yeah, okay, John, I'll be there next week for sure."

The week without a meeting was worse than normal. The irritability, restlessness and discontent would be in every conversation and every interaction the Hound had. Marie annoyed him, the kids annoyed him, and his co-workers were all idiots.

One day, he was so frustrated at work that he drove to the beer store and bought a case of beer. As the dealership was closing, he went and sat in his car, parked at the back of the lot, and started to drink.

Halfway through he had realized what he had done. It was like he was completely unaware that in light of all the consequences, he still thought it was a good idea to try to drink his problems away.

He arrived home without incident and went straight to bed. Marie never noticed.

When the Hound awoke the next morning, he was full of remorse. He felt like he had killed somebody. The guilt and self-loathing was surprisingly heavy.

Next Tuesday, he was back at the meeting, raising his hand when the chairperson asked if anyone had "gone back out," ashamedly admitting that he had to change his sobriety date, and that-once again-he only was a few days sober.

Nobody judged him. "Keep coming back," they said. "You'll get it."

This meeting was in the basement of a church. Not a very large room, with beams and posts. The Hound would arrive just a few minutes late, enter the side door, make his way to the back corner behind a post. He didn't want to speak. He did not want to be called on, to share his thoughts and feelings out loud.

The Hound didn't feel a sense of belonging to these people. Most of them were older than him, and he didn't think they were very smart either, certainly not as smart as him. Somehow, they were staying sober.

How were they doing that? The Hound couldn't figure out what he was missing. There must be some secret he didn't know yet. Some hidden key he was missing to walk through that door they had already passed through.

128

Nothing Man

The Hound found himself at a bar in the next town, alone, in the back corner, inexplicably getting drunk again.

The remorse, loneliness and feeling of failure was on him after a few beers. He knew he shouldn't be doing this. He had no idea why he was doing it again. He had no real explanation for it.

Back in the meeting on Tuesday he raised his hand again to admit his slip. "Keep coming back," they said. "You'll get it. Don't give up!"

He couldn't believe their compassion, he thought they should kick him out. Surely he was a bad example to the others.

This time the Hound got three months sober. He started to add a noon meeting when he felt overwhelmed at work. The Hound would drive downtown with his new car, in his suit to the railway station meeting. This meeting was full of rock-bottom alcoholics. Most of these folks looked like they were living on the streets. They looked disheveled, unkempt, and dirty. But when they spoke, they were elegant and soulful. The Hound learned a trick: he'd close his eyes when the meeting started, listening to the message, not judging the messenger.

He would hear things like acceptance, tolerance and surrender. "Let go and let God." "Easy does it." "One day at a time." Simple slogans—but they helped calm his mind—at least enough to get through the rest of the day without taking a drink. The meetings were working. He wasn't any better than anyone in those meetings. In fact, they had a lot to teach him.

He began to understand the word humility.

129

Street Fighting Man

One day in March, an old drinking buddy named Maurice came to town looking to celebrate his birthday.

"Take me to the pub!" he said to the Hound.

The Hound wasn't keen on this idea. "I don't wanna go in there! I'm six months sober! Why go to the barber if you don't want a haircut?"

"You don't have to drink," Maurice said, "just have a non-alcoholic beer."

This sounded harmless enough so the Hound agreed to buy Maurice a beer. As they approached the bar, Maurice ordered a pint and the Hound ordered a non-alcoholic beer.

The bartender said loudly, "We don't serve that crap here."

A table full of pretty girls overheard and started to laugh.

The Hound felt embarrassed. How could he save face? He looked on the wall behind the bartender and noticed there was a small mug. He asked the bartender "What about one of those?"

The bartender said, "Sure that's a single." And he poured the Hound a small beer.

Without a second thought, the Hound saved face but threw away six months of sobriety. Half a year of effort gone in one moment of embarrassment. He warned Maurice that this was a bad idea. Maurice laughed it off and they ordered two more, this time, full sized pints.

They went over to flirt with the girls, and an hour later they were both drunk.

The girls brushed them off, so the Hound and Maurice headed home. Marie was there, happy to see them both and was way too understanding of why the Hound was drunk again.

A few more hours of heavy drinking, and the Hound entered the black out stage of inebriation. He was still up and walking around, but there was nobody home.

He thought Maurice and Marie were being too friendly. A familiar paranoia when he'd cross the line and had more alcohol in his brain than common sense. The Hound attacked Maurice, punching him in the head. They fell against the fireplace. The Hound was like a mad dog, and Maurice scrambled away.

The fight went down the hallway and ended with Maurice unconscious in one of the rooms. The Hound went back into the living room and Marie was furious. Whenever

Marie disapproved of the Hound, it triggered a deep seated insecurity that the people who should love him didn't. It felt like betrayal and abandonment. He was dangerous in this state.

She saw the look in his eyes and as he ripped the oven door off its hinge and threw it at her, she ran out the front door into the darkness of the night.

The Hound didn't chase her. He knew he'd fucked up this time, as he staggered over, passing out on the couch.

130

Free Fallin'

He woke up in the morning and there was blood everywhere, blood on the floor, blood on the fireplace, and blood sprayed all down the walls of the hallway.

He wondered if he had killed somebody. He really didn't remember. When he found Maurice alive he panicked, his heart raced, and guilt consumed him.

Had he killed Marie?

She was alright. She had gone outside to sleep under a tree and was having a cigarette on the porch as he opened the door.

"You're an asshole," she said.

The Hound hung his head. "I'm sorry, baby. I don't know why I drank."

"Drinking is not the problem." she said. "It's you. You

are the problem."

The Hound couldn't argue. He started to clean up the evidence of his violent evening.

He kicked Maurice out and scolded him. "I warned you that was a bad idea," he muttered to himself as if to blame him.

The Hound now was adamant to redouble his efforts and to not *ever* drink again.

131

White Wedding

It's funny how time goes fast: when you look back at your life, things you thought took five years happened over five months. The passing of time feels slow when you are young. So much happens, you think it must take longer than it did.

The Hound and Marie had been through a lot in their short time together. Time really does go slow for the alcoholic and his loved ones. The five years that they spent together felt like fifty. They had moved several times, had children, made different homes, ran businesses, succeeded and failed, and had countless life-altering tragic events like most alcoholics and addicts.

The Hound loved Marie, and he wanted to show her that he was a new man. He was ready to give himself not only to God, but to her. He asked Marie to marry him. She must have really loved him, to have stayed through all this.

Marie said yes.

They decided to have their wedding in the house, just immediate family.

The Hound bought an old piano at an auction and had it delivered to the front room. Marie came from country people, and the Hound was a city boy. He thought it would be a nice touch to have her father play during the wedding.

The Hound picked a country song that he knew only her father would know, "Waltz Across Texas With Me", an old Ernest Tubb love song.

Max, who was now two, would be the ring bearer.

They invited the minister from the baptist church to perform the ceremony.

On the day of the wedding, Marie wouldn't come out of the bedroom. She was terrified. She loved him, but it was still a huge leap of faith to believe that the Hound could live up to the greater responsibility marriage required. To be the man she knew he was, deep down.

When she finally got coaxed out of the bedroom by her mother, Marie made her way down the stairs. She looked like a vision as light shone through her, like a thousand suns. She floated down the stairs, like an angel descending from Heaven.

He saw in her not just her beauty, but all the ways she saved and nourished him. In a hundred different ways, everyday. He knew that when he held her hand in his and looked into her eyes, that all was right in the world. She gave him the strength and purpose to be a man.

From this point forward, the Hound was put to rest.

The Man would take center stage.

As the minister heard their vows, the Man stood tall and promised Marie that he would work the rest of his life to be the man that she deserved. He would stay sober, be a father to the children, and the man she always knew he was.

As he leaned in to kiss her lips, he could feel her love through his fingertips. She swore to be his forever, and the Minister put it to rest.

The Man and Marie were one before God.

They couldn't afford a honeymoon, so they went to a local romantic lodge for the night. The Man stayed sober and they made love as husband and wife.

132

New Orleans Is Sinking

Things went well for a while. The Man was succeeding at work and was given an invitation to attend a special training in Tennessee. Realizing that most of the expenses would be covered, the Man decided to extend the trip for a true honeymoon with his new bride.

After the work portion of the trip finished, the Man rented a car and drove to New Orleans. He had been sober for three months again, but the closer he got to New Orleans, the more the urge to drink overtook him.

His heart raced and his skin began to crawl, he knew this feeling—he was very familiar with this state of being. Excitement filled his spine as he anticipated getting drunk—after all, it was New Orleans—the saddest city he knew. He could commiserate with it, he could wallow in his romantic pain and drown in the city of sin.

He had always viewed New Orleans as a place where

addicts and alcoholics go to die.

He couldn't wait.

He pulled into a gas station, and told Marie he was getting some beer. She looked at him sideways and said, "Are you sure?"

"Just a couple of beers, what's the harm?"

He went into the store, and the store clerk spoke with a Cajun accent that the Man could barely understand. This added to the exotic fantasy. He was in a far away land. This was an adventure. He was running through the swamp, hellhounds on his trail.

133

House of the Rising Sun

Our Man got back in the car, and offered Marie a beer. *Misery loves company,* he thought.

She took the beer but didn't open it. She looked at him like he was a child that never grew up. Her concern and disappointment were palpable.

He put the car in drive and tried not to look back in Marie's direction. He turned up the radio and opened his beer. He could smell the hops and barley. The bottle was cold between his legs and his lips were dry. Without a thought of all the misery he had put Marie through, and all the trouble he had caused himself, he tipped the bottle up in spite of it, and drank it in three big gulps.

He smacked his lips and his eyes gleamed like a cat in the night. He smiled like a villain as he tried to drag Marie along for the ride. "Here we go, baby! New Orleans!!!"

Drinking one beer after another, he couldn't get them down fast enough.

Soon, he was drunk.

He let Marie drive the last few miles into the city, as he wanted to drift away into the music and his great escape.

"There's a bar!" he pointed. "Pull in! We'll shoot a game of pool."

Marie parked the car in front of the saloon doors. They walked into a half empty, beat up, run down bar. There were dollar bills stapled on all the walls with people's signatures of where they were from. It had a pool table, smoke filled the air, and there were a few people at the bar.

This is perfect, he thought. He loved an empty bar; the loneliness of it.

A tall woman asked if the Man wanted to shoot a game.

Marie said, "Go ahead."

The Man racked the balls and the woman broke them with a bang.

He was surprised at how tall she was. Marie had gone to the bathroom and the Man asked the woman, in his drunken forwardness, "You aren't a woman, are you?"

"I'm *all* woman," she insisted.

"No way! You're way too big to be a woman."

"I'm a woman alright!"

"Prove it!"

Just then, Marie returned from the bathroom, as the woman lifted the front of her skirt and said, "Is that woman enough for ya?"

Marie couldn't believe he had gotten into that much trouble that quick. He was up to his old tricks again.

Our Man noticed Marie and said, "Honey, I was just arguing with her that she wasn't a woman, and she voluntarily showed me her thing! I'm innocent!"

Marie shook her head and didn't believe him. Soon he was trying to convince her that they should have a threesome to celebrate their honeymoon. "C'mon Marie, it'll be exciting!"

Marie was a hard "No." *Nice honeymoon,* she thought.

The drunken Man, completely oblivious of Marie's wish for a romantic getaway, continued to sell her on the idea. Marie finally had enough and dragged his sorry ass out of the bar, ready to find a hotel room for the night.

134

I'm Walkin

The Man rolled out of bed in the morning, as he sat with his elbows on his knees with his head in his hands. The hum of the air conditioner and the smell of a cheap hotel room made him feel nauseous. His head felt like there was a marching band banging off the sides of his brain. The Man was filled with guilt and terror at the blank spot in his memory of what had happened the night before.

He looked for Marie but she wasn't in the room. He half expected the tall woman from the previous night to walk out of the bathroom, but luckily it was just Marie. He quickly got up and gave her a kiss. "Let's get out of New Orleans, honey. I hate it here. This place made me drink."

Once he drank, the temptation and allure of the city disappeared like the end of a rainbow.

They piled into the car and headed out of town, pulling over by a beach on the Gulf of Mexico. Marie had a cigarette as the Man ran down to where the waves met the sand. He laid down and let the sun burn away his shame and remorse, the waves washed away the memory of yesterday's slip.

Alcoholics and drug addicts have an innate ability to wash the conscience clean quickly. They don't want to live with the remorse so they have a way to wipe it away and just move forward.

Like every alcoholic, his ability to minimize and justify his abhorrent behavior was legendary. He needed to brush it aside as fast as possible, or he would be crushed beneath the weight of a healthy conscience. The only way to continue using again was through euphoric recall: only remembering the good times.

Ten minutes of regret was all it took to wash away the shame, and he got back up and carried on with their honeymoon, as if nothing had happened.

135

The Battle Of Evermore

After returning home, the Man and Marie opened their own business. It was an idea that the Man had about creating a central locating site for used cars. He spent the next six months selling all the car dealerships on the idea. The dealers would fax their used car information into a central office, where Marie had created a database. She hired an office staff to answer the inquiries and direct clients to the dealers that had the car they wanted. It was pre-internet, so the idea was before its time.

He managed to get eight months of sobriety, but was still white knuckling it. The Man was going to the occasional AA meeting, but he didn't have a sponsor. He also didn't think it was necessary to do the steps. He certainly wasn't praying and his sobriety was precarious at best. He was staying sober on self-will, and the fear of Marie's wrath.

Their business sunk into debt and Marie and the Man were worked to the bone, their relationship became strained.

The Man was still irritable, restless and discontent. He was in full-on manic mode, trying to save his business and his dream of being rich and successful. His entire ego was wrapped up in whether it flourished or failed. He was willing to impose his egomania on anyone who stood in his way.

It was the last straw when the Man tried to interfere with how Marie was running the office in their business. She'd been putting up with his arrogance and demands long enough. The office was her domain, and she ran it wonderfully. It infuriated her that he would stick his nose in there and yell at her girls. She kicked him out of the office.

He stood there in disbelief.

Did she not realize who he was?

Marie was standing up to the Man's ego. He hated that. It overwhelmed him with rage and frustration. The Man didn't know how to handle it.

This inner conflict between his need for the love of his woman, and his desire to be in charge, came crashing down. He wanted her to be obedient, she was having none of it. Instead of becoming violent he turned and ran down the stairs. He kept running, not knowing where he was going, only that he needed to get away. Away from Marie and away from himself.

He found himself standing in the doorway of a pub.

The Man walked in slowly and could hear the laughter, the pool balls, and the music. He could smell the beer and for a second thought better of being in there. He felt like he was robbing a bank, surrounded by a swat team. He knew he couldn't leave, so it was time to take hostages. Somebody was going to pay the price. Usually it was him.

The Man had eight solid months of sobriety, but he found himself sitting in the bar with a cold pint in front of him. It was a standoff.

The Man stared down at the lager in the pint like a gunfighter facing the fastest gun in the West. He knew he was going to lose the fight, but he squinted his eyes, grit his teeth, and tried to imagine he could win the fight.

It seemed like forever. He knew as soon as he moved his hand, he was dead. He whispered to himself a soft refusal, "Don't drink it." But, he had no defense. He gave in, lifted the mug to his lips, and drank the poison. Knowing that it would only offer temporary relief from the sorrow, followed by the inevitable consequences.

The Man ordered two more and guzzled them both, desperately trying to quench his thirst. He drank himself into oblivion. This thirst could not be quenched. It wasn't his body that needed the liquid, it was his mind. The alcohol would ease him from the unbearable pain of his failure and numb his loneliness.

He drank two more.

Soon the Man was naked and standing on top of the pool table.

They quickly tackled him, made him put his pants back on, and kicked him out.

He lay on the sidewalk, trying to throw up, but couldn't.

He lay there, dry heaving, as the world spun. He felt like

a wounded animal. He couldn't get up to flee the hunter.

Then he heard Marie's voice. "What are you doing? Get in the car! I'm taking you home!"

He felt rescued. He got in the passenger's side of the family car and let her drive.

The Man opened the giant moonroof and stood on the seat, stuck his body halfway out the top of the car and started to scream at people. "Woohoo!" He pretended he was a werewolf, and shouted all sorts of obscenities at people.

They made it home and the Man staggered upstairs. He made his way across the bedroom and into the bathroom and caught his reflection in the mirror. Turning to face himself through his drunkenness, his heart fell to the floor. He looked at himself with disgust and pity. The shame knocked him to the floor. He felt incomprehensible demoralization. There he was, DRUNK, *again*.

The Man wept like a child. "Why? Why?" he cried. "Why can I not stay sober?"

In his desperate and beaten-down state, he finally surrendered.

"Help me, God, please. *Help me*."

That was December 2nd, 1993.

136

You Gotta Move

The Man awoke under the blanket, full of remorse. He could pull the blankets off him, but not the shame.

The Man remembered the old guy in the AA meeting that had lost his throat to cancer. The old guy would always say the same thing when he was asked to speak. He would hold a vibrator up to his voice box and say, *"Get on your knees and pray for sobriety."*

That morning, the Man did just that.

He slid out of bed on his stomach, so his knees would hit the ground first.

He was already uncomfortable.

The mere act of being on his knees infuriated his ego. The idea of surrendering was so foreign, but he knew he had to try it. Without gaining some humility, he didn't stand a chance. His arrogance would destroy him.

So he began to try and utter a prayer, it was as difficult as lifting a huge rock from his shoulders.

He tried to silence the critic and the scoffer in his head. It laughed at him and asked: "What are you doing? Are you really on your knees? You're such a loser! Next you'll tell me you're gonna start going to church! Get back up, buttercup! You wanna be one of *them*? A quitter?"

The Man resisted the enemy in his head. He swallowed his pride, and said his first prayer. "God?" he whispered. "If you are up there, please help me."

He sat in silence for a minute, waiting to see if he would hear an answer.

He didn't.

So he tried again. "I'm so tired. I can't stay sober. I don't want to hurt Marie anymore. Please, if you can, help me stay sober today."

This was his first prayer—at least his first prayer that he wasn't sitting on a toilet in a Texaco station. This time, he was trying to do it *before* he felt desperate.

He was trying to summon some power that would keep him from his first drink. The first drink was the one that killed him. Just like being hit by a train—it doesn't matter how many cars are behind the engine, *it's the front of the train that kills you.*

All his experience had told him that if he took a drink, it would spell disaster. He wouldn't be able to stop drinking. Then, who knows what would happen. It was like Russian roulette. He could pull the trigger, but he never knew which time he would blow his own brains out. So he pushed in all his chips and bet on God.

His hope was that somehow this silly act of getting down on his knees and asking God for help, was actually going to *work*.

He *needed* it to work. He had tried everything else.

The Man had the gift of desperation. So he forced the words from his heart. "God, please, help me stay sober today." That was all he could muster.

He jumped back to his feet and gave Marie a long hug and kiss. He said, "I know you don't want to hear this, but I'm sorry baby. I really am. I love you. You're never going to see me drunk again."

This was the first time in his life that he abandoned the idea of self-reliance. It was the first time that he consciously tried to make contact with a higher power—at least in his *adult* life. He now realized that the biggest barrier to his faith was himself—his own false narrative that he was alone, and that there was nothing that could help him; that he had to manage life on his own with cleverness and determination in order to win.

This strategy had failed him miserably. Self-reliance sounded good in theory, but in reality it created an inner world of fear. All his thoughts were consumed with how he might control everything, how to get people to behave the way he thought they should. To get from life, the things that he thought would make him whole.

The world was a complicated place. People were unpredictable, so he had given himself the title of God, with no power over anything. Of course he would be riddled with fear. He was unarmed for the battle of life. Self-reliance was a poor substitute for the all-mighty.

The Man's philosophy did not work. So how was he going to learn a completely new philosophy? How would he start to understand that he needed to have a complete psychic transformation, if he expected to avoid the same fate as he had always had?

He had constantly crashed into other people's walls; he stepped on their toes and blamed them. He expected obedience and created rebellion. He wanted loyalty but gave none. At the first hint of resistance, he grew frustrated and angry. In that state, with no other answers or ways to relieve that stress—he would drink.

The Man would drink at the uncomfortableness of not fitting into the world. Or conversely to celebrate temporary victories. He would drink for vain glory. Then he would drink again from the inevitable failures and setbacks in his life. It was a vicious cycle.

He would be riddled with resentments at even imagined slights against his omnipotent self-image, then he would drink for oblivion.

This was why he was so lonely. He never knew how to be one among many, a friend among friends. He only knew the struggle to get to the top, or fail and hide. Instead of redoubling his efforts, or taking responsibility, he would blame others, and make excuses for himself. He would become a victim and not understand why the world had not anointed him king.

He had no idea where he was going to learn all of this.

He had never been taught anything like this in school, or by his parents. The Man didn't really think that church could do it either. So, for now, he would just attend more AA meetings. Hopefully, the drunks could teach him how to live outside the bottle.

137

Changes

At the next AA meeting the Man arrived on time for a change, not trying to avoid interaction. He took a seat in front of the post, so he could be seen by all, especially the one selecting the speakers. By sitting in the front row, also referred to as "sinners' row", he was now accountable.

The meeting wound down; they announced a business meeting afterwards and suggested that members stay. Usually the Man didn't stick around, but for some reason he did this time.

They talked about who would be willing to chair a meeting, or who would volunteer for a service position, like treasurer or the one that purchased the literature.

He was a busy man, he didn't have time for those things. Then somebody brought up the necessity for someone to take over the AA meeting at the local prison. The Man glanced around the room at who might get sucked into that.

His eyes scanned the room, and he saw one hand raised.

It was his.

Who raised his hand? It couldn't have been him*!*

It must have been Divine intervention.

There it was: high up in the air. Volunteering to go to prison.

"Fantastic!" said the speaker. "You'll be great at that!"

And just like that, the Man had discovered the keys to the kingdom. He was ready to give of himself, without expecting anything in return. Now, he not only felt like a man; he knew that he was a good man.

138

Freebird

The Man even got a sponsor. Yet another guy named John. This John was a middle-aged actor. He understood the principles of the program well, and was always available when the Man needed a coffee and an understanding ear. It was time to do the Twelve Steps with purpose.

John explained to him that like thousands of recovering alcoholics before him, the Man needed to follow a path.

The first three steps were admitting he was powerless, coming to believe that there might be a power greater than him, and turning his will and life over to that power each morning. This would have to be a daily ritual for him.

Then, he was asked to put pen to paper and do his fourth step.

The fourth step required him to write a list of all his resentments, his fears, and a history of his sexual relations.

John helped him with this, as it seemed like a daunting task. After finishing his list, he carried out the fifth step with John: admitting to himself, to God, and to another human being, the true nature of his wrongdoings.

When he finished, he felt great relief. He had some self-acceptance, and, for the first time, he felt he was forgivable. His sense of God awakened.

They finished with the two prayers of step six and seven, "become willing to have God remove his defects of character, and humbly ask him to do so." For the mere act of stopping his drinking habits was only the beginning. The Man was going to need a change. He used to be a drunken horse thief, and now he was a sober one. If he expected to stay sober, he'd have to learn how to stop being a horse thief.

This was where the work began. He needed to have the willingness to let God take away the evilness from his heart, and he also needed to ask God each morning to grant that.

This would be part of his daily routine, added to his prayer each morning, along with the serenity prayer, the Lord's prayer, a prayer for his wife and family, his parents, his boss, and especially his enemies.

The Man could no longer afford resentment or even justifiable anger, for they would take him back to the drink, and the drink would kill him.

On to step eight, which required him to make a list of all the people he had harmed, and be willing to make amends to them all. Of course, it would start with Marie and the kids. After a long list of others, it would end with himself. For he had harmed many people, but the damage he had done to his own character and soul, needed forgiveness as well.

Step nine, he went to find the people he had harmed and apologized to them face-to-face. He even drove back to the old town to find the car dealer that he wronged and the friends that he had hurt along the way.

Each time he found them, his heart would race and his hands would get sweaty as he took ownership of his sins and apologized. Halfway through this, he found a new freedom, and was amazed by it. For the first time in his life he felt a true sense of humility. Not a negative emotion like eating humble pie, but an exhilarating freedom from his ego. He felt at one with himself, his fellows, and God.

He was alone no more.

139

Stairway To Heaven

Steps ten, eleven and twelve were what they called the "living steps". They would be practiced daily for the rest of his life.

Step ten required him to take personal inventory of his behavior and, when he was wrong, promptly admit it.

This would take ongoing humility as he was frequently wrong. It was worth it, though. Making the amends over and over again for his poor behavior worked as an inspiration to change. He wanted God to help him change into somebody that wouldn't have to make so many amends.

Step eleven, he continued with prayer and meditation to improve his conscious contact with the God of his understanding.

The Man did his prayer every morning, asking how he could help the alcoholic who was still sick and how he could be a channel of God's light and love.

That he might understand what God would wish of him, then have the power to carry it out.

"Show me the way, Lord."

The Man also spent a few minutes every day in silence, mostly reflecting on all that he had to be grateful for. Praying was talking to God and meditation was listening.

Be still, and know that I am God.

Finally, step twelve, having had a spiritual awakening as a result of these steps, he would carry this message to those that still suffered, and practiced the principles in *all* of his affairs.

The Man would dedicate himself to carrying the message of hope, the AA program, and God's love.

He would attend many AA meetings and work with newcomers and those who hadn't grasped the solution yet. Understanding and interpreting the literature would help many who were lost find the error of their ways. The Man would spend countless hours before and after the AA meetings sharing his wisdom and love with those who needed it. He sponsored many men and shared his faith and the path he took to find and unite with the Lord.

This was not enough. He still had a wife and family that deserved a loving husband and father. This meant that he spent time being of service to them. Time was the greatest gift, to be a calm and loving presence in their life. To listen and help humbly without preaching or forcing himself into areas of their life that were theirs to discover. Allowing them to be wrong and loving them in spite of it, waiting patiently for them to ask him for guidance. Setting a good example of the joyful life of sobriety and recovery.

He had financial obligations to meet and started to to practice these principles in all his affairs. To have a heart of service, humility, patience, tolerance, and love with his work colleagues and clients.

The AA program was not a theory. *He had to live it.*

140

You Don't Have to Live Like A Refugee

Every morning the Man got on his knees. He was getting less uncomfortable with it as his humility grew and his ego shrunk. "God, help me stay sober today."

Those simple six words said in earnest, he believed, was the foundation of recovery.

Up to his feet he'd spring and off to conquer the world.

He worked hard as a salesman and sales manager providing for his family. He had no debt, and felt no urge to drink. The prayer was working. Every morning he was on his knees, and a new bounce in his step was emerging, propelling him forward.

Marie took a job as an accountant and they became a dual-income family.

The Man and Marie were finally flush.

141

Digging In the Dirt

Things had become so solid, the Man became comfortable enough to reach out to his parents.

His parents were looking to retire and the Man helped them find a new house, right down the street from him. In this newfound persona, he was finally able to become a good son. He had learned through his own recovery, that whoever they were in the past, they had done the best they could with what they knew. They had both come from much harder upbringings, and a much tougher time.

His mother was raised by an alcoholic, who returned from World War Two and became abusive. Her father would stagger home from the bar and she would hide in the closet. She knew what was coming, her father was abusive and violent towards her mother when he was drunk. When he sobered up in the morning he'd say how much he loved her. The word "love" didn't mean anything to her. This was probably why she never told her son she loved him. She left home at fifteen and soon joined the military, where she met the Man's father.

The Man's father came from an alcoholic mother, who chased off his father and married another alcoholic, a step father who hated the children. The Man's father never learned how to be a father, leaving his home at fourteen.

Trauma is generational. It gets passed down for the children to learn how to deal with.

With his newfound compassion for his parents, the Man was able to help them in their recovery, by loving them unconditionally. They became closer than ever.

The Man's brother was drinking alcohol himself now and the Man patiently loved him, until his brother was ready to quit himself. His brother was affected differently from childhood; he was much more intellectual and spent most of his life strategizing his destiny, using alcohol to quiet his mind, drinking himself into complete isolation. The Man would never give up on him. He loved his only brother. Years later, they shared the journey of sobriety together and became the best of friends.

The family could feel the new atmosphere in the house. Though Jessica was a rebellious teenager, she began to trust her parents again. Marcus excelled at rugby and had a host of friends. Young Max was the love-child, and had never seen the Man drunk.

Marie returned to baking and was the rock of the family. She held everybody blend together with her wisdom and her love.

142

I Walk The Line

That Wednesday night, the Man met another AA man who had been doing the meetings in the jail. In the parking lot outside the prison they joined together and approached the prison gate.

It was raining hard like it did most days in the winter on the west coast.

They buzzed the control tower. Nothing.

They buzzed it again. A crackle came through the speaker: "Hello, how can I help you?"

"We're here to put on the AA meeting."

"Okay, come register at the office." The door clicked open as they entered the first set of gates. They approached the second gate, a barbed wire fence, 18-feet high.

The speaker made a crackle. "Look up into the camera."

As they both glanced up through the night rain, the men heard the second door click open.

They pushed their way into the prison yard. They were in General Population now; they were amongst the inmates.

The Man tried to look tough as he walked with the AA man across the yard to the office. He realized that at this moment, he had no protection. Somebody could stab him, or beat him, but he trusted that God was protecting him.

They showed their ID and signed in, making their way down the hallway to a room used for the meeting. The announcement came over the PA system.

"AA meeting, AA meeting in room 301."

The Man anxiously awaited to see who would come and sit at the table with them. The door swung open and a man in an orange jumpsuit walked in. He was tall and lean. The tattoos on his hands told a story of broken dreams. The beard on his face was patchy and thin. The look in his eyes was mean, yet afraid. He stared across the table as if the AA men were an enemy about to feed him. He was hungry for what they had but mistrusting in what he might have to do to get it.

Another man came in, shorter, rounder, but with a different look in his eyes. A thousand-yard stare, as he looked right through you without making eye contact.

Soon there were ten inmates, all sitting, glaring suspiciously at the outsiders.

"Welcome," said the AA man. "My name's Al, and I'm an alcoholic. Thank you for coming."

The Man spoke up, introducing himself as an alcoholic. "Welcome to the Wednesday night AA meeting."

They began the session by reading the serenity prayer and then gave each person a copy of *Alcoholics Anonymous*, the main literature for AA. They each took turns reading. Some of the inmates read fluently, while others struggled with simple words.

At the end of the reading, the Man shared his story. He told them he was still fairly new at continuous sobriety, as he had several slips over the past few years, but he knew that this was the last "house on the block," that the answer lay within these pages and in the rooms of AA. He was committed to do whatever it took to stay sober.

The Man explained that he had volunteered to take over this meeting, and that he would be here every Wednesday, come rain or shine.

As the inmates began to share, they all seemed quite touched that the Man would give his time. They were grateful for his truth-telling of his own struggles.

They ended the meeting with a prayer and the Man left the prison, excited that he finally found somewhere he belonged: his ego believed he found people to help—people who needed him, people who were less fortunate than him, and his humility began to grow through the service of others.

He was so affected positively by this experience that in no time he was going twice a week and never missed a meeting for six years.

For he knew that he was the one that was getting the most from this commitment. The giving of himself with no expectation of return was transforming his heart and showing him the way to have self-worth.

143

Into The Mystic

Some of the Man's new AA friends came over weekly for mediation. The Man started to seek God. He learned about Sufis, and read *The Autobiography of a Yogi*. He became a vegetarian and even tried reading the Quran and the *Bhagavad Gita*.

Soon he was doing breathing exercises and chanting *Laaaaa-Oooo-mmmm*. During one of these meditations, once the chanting had stopped, he sat in silence and for the first time in his life he felt the loving presence of God.

God was a feeling. God felt like peace and serenity. The Man felt safe and loved in His presence. In the dark silence he could hear God whispering, "I love you," over and over.

He finally understood the kind of love that God could give. It was the kind of love he looked for his whole life. It was the feeling that he thought he would get at the bottom of every bottle, after taking every drug, or sleeping with every woman. His search was over. He had finally quenched his eternal thirst.

When the session ended he thanked the guru and hugged him deeply. He raced home to tell Marie of his experience. This began our Man's eternal quest for God consciousness.

The Man studied the seven chakras and had a mantra for each one. He would end on the crown chakra with a thousand rays of white light streaming down through the top of his head, as he sat cross-legged floating down as a slow moving river on a giant lotus flower.

He was becoming "enlightened."

144

Higher Love

This was going to be a problem. He had a wife, three kids, and bills to pay. He couldn't go sit on top of the mountain. The addictive behavior had migrated to spiritual pride. He started to walk around completely unaffected by anyone or anything. He felt peace, but this peace was gained at a cost; the cost of being truly present in his life or having any empathy. He had swung the pendulum too far to the spirit. In this state, he was more detached than he was useful. Inner peace is grand, but not at the cost of his true life. He still had much to accomplish on his earthly plane.

He wanted his religion to be more complex and sophisticated, as he became more and more pious.

He was driving Marie crazy and even talked of abstaining from sex.

That was the last straw for Marie, she cooked a pan of bacon and told him: "Eat the bacon and take me to bed, or else I'm leaving!"

The Man knew she was right. He was using spirituality to escape. It wasn't much different than being drunk. Just a lot less fun for Marie.

The next morning, on his knees, he had the realization that he had been denying Christ; for if he prayed to Christ he would be a servant. He wanted to be a spiritual giant. He intellectualized and sought a faith that would raise him above others. Through Christ he would have to learn how to wash feet. After all, the one God that appeared to him and saved him was Christ the redeemer—why would he not pray to *Him*?

Up until then, he thought the Christ believers were weak, sucked into going to church and paying money.

These judgements had blocked him from the love he needed, as his intellectual ideas were keeping him from true faith.

He decided he would try to be humble enough to ask Jesus for help; he would make the effort to return to the man who appeared before him in his darkest hour as a spirit of light: *"Believe in me, and all will be well."*

The Man apologized in his prayer. "Forgive me, Jesus, I've denied you and rejected you, when you were the one that saved me. Take my spiritual pride from me. I will now seek to know you and to do your will."

145

Simple Man

Every morning the Man prayed to Jesus. He still did his yoga and meditation, but he began to study the teachings of Jesus. The red letters in the Bible were the words that Jesus spoke, and the Man studied them. They spoke to his heart and he saw the truth within them.

The Man's favorite teaching was about the kind of humility that was needed to let God enter your heart.

"A man asked Jesus, 'Who is the most powerful person in heaven?' and Jesus called forth a child, and said, 'Until your faith can be like this child's, you cannot enter the kingdom of heaven.'" This was beautiful to the Man. It spoke to his spiritual pride. Trying to float above everybody on his intellect and complicated religions. Unless he could approach God with the vulnerability of a child he could not gain the humility needed for the love of God to enter his heart.

The Man discovered that heaven was here and now.

Heaven could be attained through God consciousness. The understanding that through this surrender of ego the spirit of the light could enter his heart and he would know peace. The Man had already lived in hell: hell to him was the absence of God. So in the presence of God he was in heaven.

He also loved when Jesus explained, "The greatest among you shall be a servant." For he now understood that greatness could only be attained through the service of others; that the one who was lucky enough to understand this, would be free from fear and self pity. The servant could be a channel of God's light and love to others. Through this kind of service, he would be full of that love and light. So full, that his cup would runneth over.

The giving of oneself with no expectation of return, was the will of God and would bring him to heaven while he still lived here on earth.

Every time he talked with a newcomer, or a still-suffering alcoholic, he explained this sacred truth and the spirit would be with him. He could feel the love in the air. This was *his* gift, his faith was its own reward.

What he once thought as a weakness, he now knew was *strength*. Jesus showed him the way. He was the Lord but he spent his time teaching and serving those that needed it. The Man saw this as the secret to a life of freedom: that true power came in the ability to let the Lord's love shine through you.

He now started to understand the teachings and example of Christ. The principles of love and tolerance, forgiveness and patience, acceptance, charity, and the giving of oneself to the service of others. Practicing these principles would now be his lifetime quest.

be his lifetime quest.

146

The Rising

The Man did two meetings a week in jail, plus a couple on the outside, to help him fit into regular society.

The Man didn't hide behind the post anymore. He was happy to share his experience, strength, and hope and even took up to washing the dishes, which was mostly getting lipstick off of coffee cups. This act of service helped him feel a sense of belonging within the group. It ensured that he'd stay for the prayer and the fellowship that occurred after the meeting, as he needed this to overcome his shyness with strangers.

This would teach the Man how to act in social settings, without drinking. When he felt uncomfortable, he would get up and start to help. In helping and serving he could get out of his own self-centered fear and start to feel okay in his own skin. Serving others gave him belonging.

The Man wanted to feel the presence of God, to live

peacefully and happily. He now knew that he must dedicate the rest of his life to the service of God, and shining his light and love to those who were still lost.

The jail had freed him from the bondage of himself. He knew for sure that he had found the answer: that to give, was to receive. This was the key to life; this was the secret of love.

147

Grace, Too

Years later, the Man had a job opportunity that would take him to a different country. He handed over the responsibilities of the jail meetings to another AA member.

Our new Man woke up daily, got on his knees to say his prayers of gratitude and offered himself to the service of the Lord. He carried this attitude of love and tolerance in all his affairs. He became a better husband and father; a better son and brother. He ran his businesses like a trusted servant, helping the clients and his employees with kindness.

He became many people's AA sponsor: helping people to admit their problem and to seek help from Alcoholics Anonymous. He worked tirelessly with many newcomers, helping them understand the steps and the process of recovery to reduce their ego to allow God's light to shine within them.

In his last meeting with the inmates, many of whom had

now become his friends, he thanked them for allowing him to be of service and for giving him the opportunity to share AA's message of love and hope. They each took turns hugging him, expressing gratitude, and wishing him well.

The Man welled up with emotion and gratitude, and as he left the prison that day, he heard the gate lock behind him. He broke down and cried in joy and gratitude for what he had been given. He understood that the man he once was, belonged in jail, and that through the grace of God, and Alcoholics Anonymous, he was finally able to walk free.

He now knew what Jesus meant when he said "Drink of me and you shall *thirst* no more."

EPILOGUE

Ode To Joy

The Man went on to help hundreds of alcoholics find AA, sharing his journey towards faith. He managed to stay sober for more than thirty years, and is still happily married to Marie, after 38 years and counting.

Their three children gave them five grandchildren.

Marie and the Man achieved great success in business as well. They went on to build a multi-million dollar business in Mexico and live a life of financial independence. A credit to Marie, his faith in Jesus, and his service in *Alcoholics Anonymous*.

The Man has written this story to share his journey from childhood through addiction to redemption, so that it may help others. We hope you, or someone you love, will read this book and find the way to freedom.

"Abandon yourself to God as you understand God. Admit your faults to Him and to your fellows. Clear away the wreckage of your past. Give freely of what you find and join us. We shall be with you in the Fellowship of the Spirit, and you will surely meet some of us as you trudge the Road of Happy Destiny."

— Alcoholics Anonymous, p.164

"The child doesn't get trauma from pain, but from suffering the pain alone"

— *Gabor Maté*

Author's Note

The addict/alcoholic must first admit their situation, truthfully. First to themselves, and then to others. They must develop a faith in a higher power that will lead them out of this hell of alone-ness. Then a house cleaning is required. Wrongs made right. Fences mended. And a new daily effort to do the will of their higher power. To treat others with love and tolerance, and to find people worse-off than them to carry the message of love and recovery.

If this is done, with half the effort that the alcoholic or addict puts into their use, then they will recover quickly and great things will come to pass for them and countless others. They will feel a sense of belonging and understand the word *serenity*. They will know peace. They will understand the secret to happy living. This is a great fact for them.

Alcoholics Anonymous is not the only path to recovery, but it has proven to be effective. There are AA meetings all around the world. In every town and city. Millions of recovered addicts and alcoholics are in them, eagerly willing to help the next person that finds their way to their door.

This book's primary purpose is to carry this message to the alcoholic that still suffers. And to point the way to the path of redemption. May God keep you and guide you to your true destiny.

H. W. Terrance

Get the Playlist!

The Hound's Hits
(Thirst Playlist)

Link: playlist.thirstnovel.com

List of Resources

AA: www.aa.org

NA: www.na.org

Al-Anon: www.al-anon.org

Codependents Anonymous: www.coda.org

Adult Children of Alcoholics: www.adultchildren.org

Sex Addiction: www.sa.org

Suicide Prevention: www.helpguide.org

Family Abuse: www.familyabusecenter.org

Spousal Abuse: www.ncadv.org

Drug Addiction: www.drugaddiction.org

About the Author

The author is not important, it is the message that matters. The message of God's love; that nobody is irredeemable. All people make mistakes. It's never too late to be forgiven and to turn one's life around to serve God and your fellows.

Milton Keynes UK
Ingram Content Group UK Ltd.
UKHW050301030924
447802UK00007B/511

9 798330 366750